Carissa Ann Lynch is the *USA Today* and *Wall Street Journal* bestselling author of *My Sister Is Missing*, *Without a Trace*, *Like Follow Kill*, *The One Night Stand*, *She Lied She Died*, *Whisper Island*, *The Secrets of Cedar Farm*, the *Flocksdale Files* trilogy, the *Horror High* series, *Searching for Sullivan*, *This Is Not About Love*, *Midnight Moss*, and *Shades and Shadows*. She resides in Floyds Knobs, Indiana, with her partner, children, and collection of books. With a background in psychology, she has always been a little obsessed with the darker areas of the mind.

carissaannlynch.wordpress.com

facebook.com/CarissaAnnLynchauthor
twitter.com/carissaannlynch
instagram.com/carissaannlynch_thrillers

Also by Carissa Ann Lynch

My Sister is Missing

Without a Trace

Like, Follow, Kill

The One Night Stand

She Lied She Died

Whisper Island

The Secrets of Cedar Farm

The Bachelorette Party

THE SUMMER SHE DISAPPEARED

CARISSA ANN LYNCH

One More Chapter
a division of HarperCollins*Publishers*
1 London Bridge Street
London SE1 9GF
www.harpercollins.co.uk
HarperCollins*Publishers*
Macken House, 39/40 Mayor Street Upper,
Dublin 1, D01 C9W8

This paperback edition 2023

First published in Great Britain in ebook format
by HarperCollins*Publishers* 2023
Copyright © Carissa Ann Lynch 2023
Carissa Ann Lynch asserts the moral right to be identified
as the author of this work
A catalogue record of this book is available from the British Library

ISBN: 978-0-00-851142-5

Printed and bound in the UK using 100% Renewable Electricity
by CPI Group (UK) Ltd

To Shannon, Dexter, Tristian, and Violet—thanks for your love and support.

Violet…you're too young to read my books (thankfully), but you'll be happy to know that your obsession with Titanic spilled onto the pages of my work and seeped into this story. Thanks for the inspiration, as always.

I wonder if, in the dark night of the sea, the octopus dreams of me.

N. Scott Momaday

Chapter One

WANT TO SEE A DEAD BODY?

CURRENT DAY

There is a body in the bedroom closet.

Those were the words of the construction worker, the only female on the team.

Cindy. The woman's name is Cindy, I chastised myself.

I'd always been good with faces, terrible with names. And still, I didn't know most of the locals in Hillendale, much less the burly construction and home improvement crew I'd hired to work on my parents' lake house. *My house. It's my house now,* I reminded myself.

Cindy's words spun like a cyclone. Words buzzing in my brain, growing louder...

There is a body in the bedroom closet.

That can't be what she said. I must have simply misheard…

I followed the wooden planks of the foot bridge, eyes forward and hands firm on the gnarly, old handrails. By the time I reached the other side of the lake, feet anchored in the rich black soil of the forest, Cindy's garbled words had been reduced to nonsensical syllables in my brain.

I must have heard wrong. The connection was poor…

Halloween was still weeks away, too early for pranks. And Cindy didn't strike me as the trickster type. I'd only met her on two occasions, crossing paths on my first morning at the site and again last week when I did a surprise drop-by to check on the workers' progress. Cindy had stood out to me; of course she had, being the only woman in the group.

She seemed like a quiet woman, barely twenty, her eyes cast low, focused on her work as she poured a smooth, flat layer of concrete for the new patio. She was pretty, muscular but not too much so … not like what you'd expect.

I shouldn't expect anything. It's not that weird, seeing an attractive young woman in that role, is it?

But tonight, Cindy had sounded different, her voice crackling on the other end of the line, her voice *frantic*, cutting hard as stone, raising to a feverish pitch as she

2

relayed what she'd found at the small lake house my parents left me.

When the call came in, I was sitting in front of the television with the volume on low. That was the way I spent most nights since moving to the town of Hillendale after inheriting the lake house and leaving my husband Jason behind. A weathered paperback strewn across my lap; remnants of a TV dinner balanced lazily on the arm of the sofa; Jimmy Fallon's voice so low I had to strain my ears to catch the punchlines ... that's when the call came in.

"You have to come! Come right now," Cindy barked down the line.

That's when her voice turned to static, and that's when I knew—service at the lake house at 1 Daisy Lane was the worse—so terrible, that the crew claimed it was a "dead zone", and they often traveled to neighboring properties to make their calls, or to check their Twitter feeds.

"There's a body in the bedroom closet," she said, her voice fading in and out. And before I could ask her to repeat herself, she was gone.

The path curled through a tunnel of trees, cedar and pine. Then it split. *Left or right, west or east? Pick your poison, my dear,* Kathi Jo's words came back to me, fluttering like moth wings, beating on my inner ear.

It was a moonless night, the kind that swallows up everything. The kind that makes you afraid of the dark.

West. West is best, of course, the memory of Kathi Jo followed me up the hilltop. I didn't need a light to find my way to the lake house. *My house. It's my house now.*

I could have walked the wooded trail with my eyes closed, even now, all these years later.

The wind howled, the night air freezing. The sort of cold that pierces bone and turns skin to goose flesh. I was underdressed, in a Grateful Dead t-shirt and ripped blue jeans, but I'd had the sense, at least, to put on thick socks and my hiking boots before leaving my apartment.

I followed the east trail past the creek, around a thick black boulder that looked like Bigfoot hunched in the dark. I brushed the boulder's cold, slick surface with my fingers as I passed. *For luck. Always touch for luck …*

Over the hill, the lake house came into view.

Even now, thirty-something years later, the place still felt like home to me in so many ways…

There was nothing special about the lake house. In fact, some might call it downright ugly. A simple salt box at the edge of the forest, its sloped roof made of timber. Inside, the decorum from another era—or perhaps another life, altogether. A stag's head over the fireplace; a beaver and a large-mouthed bass on the wall. The furniture, all eighties styled … forever stuck in a forgotten era, when life was easier. Better.

It was a drafty old house, water stains on the ceilings. A cobweb for every corner. The sort of place reserved for slasher flicks and murder mysteries.

It used to give me chills, coming here as a child ... but, slowly, the whole place grew on me—not the place, but the memories. Mama in her reading chair, skin soft and tissue-thin. Dad on the back deck, watching the lake through a gap in the forest.

See anything new, Daddy?

Nope. It's always the same. Peaceful. Unchanging. And that's why I love it here. The years go by, but the lake stands still. Nothing in Hillendale ever changes, Daddy would say.

A sliver of moonlight revealed itself, casting the lake house in spooky shadows, like something from a haunted house. The shadows around the forest grew longer, stretching endlessly in the dark.

Oh, but it did change, Dad. And it happened when I least expected it. Nothing stays the same, Dad, not even here ... especially *not here ... surely, deep down, you knew that, too.*

For the first time since returning to Lake Hillendale, I felt a flash of fear in my chest.

This place isn't safe. Too many dreadful things happened here, things I'll never forget.

As Cindy emerged from the front of the house, it occurred to me, for the first time, that she had no business being here. Not at this time of night.

Why was she working this late, at half-past midnight?

The crew often showed up early on weekdays, retiring by four or five. Her presence here was uncanny, and she appeared to be all alone as she approached me in the dark.

Silent and weightless, this gazelle-like creature with forearms like boulders sauntered toward me. She looked bigger, stronger, than I had initially realized. Perhaps meeting her alone was a mistake, something I never would have done had it been one of her male counterparts asking me to come.

I should have called the police after receiving her call. That would have been the smart thing to do...

"There you are. Thank God you came." Cindy stepped into the moonlight; cigarette clinched between her teeth. She looked decades older than I remembered.

"I-I'm sorry," I told her. "The connection was bad. I couldn't hear your words, what you were saying..."

Cindy tossed the cigarette in the brush, opened her mouth, and repeated those dreadful words again. The ones I didn't want to hear; the ones she had shouted earlier into the phone.

"There is a body in the bedroom closet. I'm sorry if I was freaked out on the phone, ma'am, but I didn't know what else to do. It looks like it's been there a while. I got ... I got scared."

But she didn't look scared at all.

I walked toward the front door of the lake house, my brain pinwheeling. This made no sense at all.

The only body that comes to mind…

Cindy was talking, directing me where to go. But it was another voice I heard, playful in my mind.

I could almost hear her—the ghost of Kathi Jo—her singsong voice floating on the wind.

Her lips tickling my earlobe: *Want to see a dead body?*

SUMMER OF '98

The first time I went to Lake Hillendale, I was only a few months old. I don't remember it, obviously, but those later years of my youth are seared into my brain. Riding my trike, pumping little legs around the cul-de-sac in front of my grandmother's house. Kathi Jo and the others … those late, sticky nights in Hillendale…

The lake house belonged to my father's mother and then it belonged to my parents.

Mom and Dad rented a pontoon boat one summer, strapping me in so tight that half my face disappeared in the life jacket, gasping for air. *Always gasping for air at that age.*

My early memories of the lake house were hazy, and mostly good. But that all changed the summer I turned thirteen. The summer of Kathi Jo Redfield.

The funny thing about those years ... the way Mom and Dad talked about our yearly vacations made me feel like a spoiled little princess. The lake house, the boat, the way the water of Lake Hillendale glistened and shone like glass ... the way they told it, it was something out of a fairytale.

It wasn't a fancy vacation destination. Just a drafty old house that belonged to my grandmother, two hours from our double wide trailer in Branton. But since my parents owned it outright, it was the perfect family destination each summer.

For a while, I felt like royalty at the lake house. Like the luckiest girl in the world...

While my friends went to Europe and the Caribbean, or to Florida or South Carolina, every year, we drove a hundred miles west to Lake Hillendale.

Every year, it was just Dad, Mom, and me. We stayed at the house; it was our yearly adventure. Some years Dad rented a boat for a few days, so we could go out and swim and fish in the brackish-green waters of Lake Hillendale. Some years we couldn't afford it.

Most nights, we would gather round the fire pit, roasting hot dogs, and sticky marshmallows. Watching the logs turn from ash to dust. I wrote stories in my notebook and sometimes, when I could get one or both of my parents to listen, I shared them. Always frightening, always dark—always a bit of truth laced in the margins, between the lines of my stories...

You're a real mood killer, Willow, my mother said once, when she drank too much beer and brandy. That was the last time I shared one of my stories with her.

I would walk through the woods, during the day, mostly. Stumbling down the rocky hillside, following the path by memory. *Down, down, down* until I reached the water.

At the edge of the muddy shoreline, there was an old stone staircase that led down into the water. Only the first couple steps were visible; the rest underwater, mossy and dark, like the entrance to a crumbly, cursed pool, or an ancient underwater cavern.

I would travel down the steps slowly, trying to anchor my feet to the stone for as long as I could, trying to see how deep I could take them underwater, but I always floated up before reaching the bottom.

The inside of the house was a creamy egg-shell blue. I hated the dead animals on the walls at first: the stag and the beaver; the angry eagle. Their glass eyes black and warning, watching me all the time. The animals came with the house, apparently. Just something we had to live with during our summers. Because Dad refused to let Mom take them down after Grandma passed away.

I hated those animals. But then I liked to remind myself of fairytales. Fairytales are rarely pretty, not when you strip them down to their bones. Snow White, or *Sneewittchen* as she was called in the original story, the German one, was saved by a rugged huntsman. I liked to imagine the house were his, these animals his trophies. And in this freezing cold house on the edge of the forest covered in vines, with the dead creatures on the wall and the green-black waters and the mossy rooftop with its green cloud cover ... that it is where we fall in love in my story. That is where the hunter restrains himself, refusing to cut out my beating heart as a prize for the evil queen. *Take that, Wicked Queen!*

Grandma had kept the place sparsely furnished, a threadbare couch in one corner, a Lazy Boy chair in the other. There was a dining area, small kitchenette, and the main bedroom reserved for my parents.

Then, upstairs, upstairs was my world. A loft, the ceiling so low and slanted that I'd hit my head if I stood up straight. And the big mattress on the floor with the burly old blankets, my own little summer nest.

I liked it up there, stretched out on my back, thighs sticky with sweat because the AC didn't reach that high, watching the lake water swirl back and forth, back and forth, from my balcony view of the water. Glittery and magical, the image like a silent lullaby.

When the house was quiet, and I was sure my parents were sleeping, I'd go out on the balcony and lie flat on my back, trying to avoid splinters while I counted the stars. Thinking about boys. Touching myself; even, once, going as far as to get fully undressed, the moonlight my only spectator.

Luckily, I was fully clothed on the first night I saw Kathi Jo Redfield. I wish I could say the same for her.

Flat on my back, I turned my head to the side, looking out over the water. The sideways view was disorienting from the balcony, my world tipped on its side like a tilt-o-whirl.

Something was stirring out there ... a change in the wind or a rustle in the trees, so succinct that I couldn't put my finger on it.

But that's when I saw it.

Something. No ... *someone*.

Someone was out there, head bobbing in the water. For a moment, I let the fantasies take hold. A mermaid. No, a *merman*. A Loch Ness Monster that transforms into a sexy young siren...

But this was no mythical beast. Dark tendrils of hair swirled around her head. And she was coming closer, and closer still ... lifting herself from the water, body glittering in the cool night air, as she slowly ascended the stone staircase, one step at a time, and entered the muddy banks of the deep dark lake.

Cattails parted as she moved up the hillside, gliding over the rocky terrain and zigzagging through the brush. Then, suddenly, she was standing in my own backyard, water dripping in rivulets down her naked body.

All this time, watching her emerge like a ghostly maiden, I hadn't moved a muscle. I was still sprawled on my backside, cheek pressed flat to the wooden slats of the decking, barely breathing.

The girl stopped in the center of the yard, hands resting on the grooves of her curvy hip bones. She was neither woman nor girl, but like me, stuck in that awful in-between. But she was nothing like the girls from Parker Valley Middle School. Even in the dark, I could tell.

I could see the glint of her piercings. Five holes in each ear, a hoop spread over both nostrils, like an angry bull. Eyes large, blue maybe … and she had choppy black hair, wet and plastered to her skull.

There was something black on her left thigh, too, a large tattoo … something angry and tentacled. She reminded me of a big wet butterfly, a specimen under glass.

The girl cleared her throat, stood her ground. It was then that my chest seized with terror. Surely, she couldn't see me all the way up here in the dark…

"Take a picture. It'll last longer," she crooned, her voice soft but raspy.

My lips parted to say something, perhaps to apologize … but I found that my mouth was full of bees.

I couldn't see her smile in the dark, but I could hear it when she said, "Yoo-hoo, I see you up there."

My eyes squeezed shut, my cheeks blazed with embarrassment. Although, it made no sense; it was she who was trespassing, she who was naked ... why did I feel like a creepy voyeur?

"Fine. Just lie there then," she sighed, bored with me now.

I heard movement in the grass, twigs snapping. I kept my eyes closed, held my breath, forced myself to count to 100. And when I opened them, she was gone. As though she'd never been there to begin with, just a butterfly of the lake, another piece of my homespun fairytale.

～

I woke to the smells of my mother's cooking. Eggs, over easy. Bacon, burned. And, maybe, jam on toast today. I sat up on my mattress, stretching, trying to reach the top of the loft with the tips of my fingers from where I sat on the bed. And that's when I remembered: the girl.

I took my time getting dressed. Everything at this age felt like effort, too much. I shimmied into a pair of jean shorts. Tugged a Rolling Stones t-shirt over my head.

By the time I plodded downstairs and slunk through the living room to the kitchen, hoping for coffee, I'd forgotten the girl again. But then, there she was. Standing in the middle of my parents' summer kitchen. Not a nighttime phantom, not an apparition. She was a real-life girl.

"There she is!" My mother was wearing her fake smile, the one she reserved for guests.

"Willow, this is Kathi Jo and her mom, Isabella! This is my daughter, Willow."

Kathi Jo looked different in the light of day, no longer the midnight harpy. Her choppy black waves were tucked back in a tight ponytail at the base of her neck. Her face looked softer, a splattering of freckles on her nose and cheeks. Her mother, on the other hand, looked nothing like her: short and curvy where Kathi Jo was graceful and tall and hair white-blonde, straight as a pin.

"Hi there," I said, quietly. I could feel the harpy staring, studying me. But I refused to meet her eye. *Again, why do I feel like I did something wrong? She's the weirdo, standing buck naked in my backyard,* I questioned myself.

There was a long pause, awkward and strained. My mother jumped to fill that space.

"We are thrilled to finally have some neighbors! I mean, we don't live here year-round, but we summer here every ... well, summer," my mother said. My mother was an awkward woman, despite how hard she tried not to be.

Standing next to Kathi Jo's mother, my mother looked like a round little troll. My mother, with her glasses and tiny white teeth. She fluttered around the kitchen with nervous anxiety, talking to our guests.

"Ah. So, this is just your summer home?" the woman asked, giving my mother a sly smile then looking at me. I rolled my eyes, looking around for my father to save me.

I waited for my mother to tell them that this was actually our grandmother's house and we lived in the Branton trailer park in Boone County. But she decidedly failed to mention that part.

"Ummm ... sort of," my mother said.

I cut in, "Did you just move here?" I looked at the woman, eyes sliding over to look at the girl. *Kathi Jo. Sounds like a redneck name to me*, I thought.

"Yeah, we bought the house next door." Kathi Jo jabbed a thumb, indicating the big, gingerbread-looking stone house to the left of ours. I'd seen people staying there on occasion during the summer, usually groups of young adults who partied too loud and pissed my parents off. They never would have agreed to live in Hillendale year-round, even if Dad's factory job were closer. *It's a place for summer, not for a real life*, they would say. And I often got the impression that they looked down on the permanent families, at least the ones who lived full-time in the small cottages and rentals.

"Are you living year-round then?" my mother asked them, hiding her judgement well.

The woman smiled. I liked her name better than her daughter's. *Isabella.* A pretty name.

"That's the plan. It's just Kathi Jo and I. I love to kayak, and I used to live here with my family on the other side of the lake. Being here feels like home."

"Willow, why don't you take a walk with Kathi Jo, let us grown-ups talk? You can show her the path down to the lake in case she likes to go swimming," my mother said.

I could barely conceal my amusement. Covering my mouth with my hand, I glanced over at Kathi Jo; she wiggled both brows, the corner of her lips hinting at a smile.

"Sure. Why not? Do you like to go swimming?" I asked.

"Definitely," Kathi Jo said, grinning. She had a nice smile, like something out of a magazine.

Our mothers were watching as we high-tailed it through the kitchen, snaking through the slide-in screen off the back porch.

Kathi Jo burst into giggles as soon as we stepped outside. I held up one finger to my lips. Dad was somewhere nearby.

"Morning, there!" Dad said.

Kathi Jo started, and I squeezed her arm jovially, snorting with glee.

"Morning, Dad. Just going for a walk with our new

16

neighbor." Dad was sprawled out in a plastic deck chair, his feet propped up on the seat of another chair, his cup of decaf in one hand and a Clancy paperback in the other.

"We have neighbors?" he asked, flicking a page. His eyes were red, and he looked hung over.

"Yep." Kathi Jo and I brushed past him, heading for the woods. I led the way, curling around the behemoth rock, brushing it for luck on my way by.

I glanced back just in time to see Kathi Jo doing the same.

As we skirted through the woods, I was sweating. Even with the canopy of trees overhead, I could tell the sun was going to be reckless today. By the end of summer, the grass would be crunchy and brown beneath my feet, my skin tanned dark as leather before returning to school in Branton.

We waited until we had reached the clearing and were out of earshot, before speaking.

Kathi Jo laughed so hard she had to bend at the waist. I kicked off my sneakers and socks, chuckling too.

"First time seeing the lake, huh?" I teased.

"First time during the daytime, I guess," Kathi Jo said. "Why did you ignore me last night when I called out to you? I could see you there on the balcony, plain as day. Were you pretending to be asleep?"

A flutter of shame tickled my belly, remembering how

embarrassed I'd felt last night. I shook it off, again reminding myself that she was the one caught skinny-dipping like a midnight maiden.

I told the truth: "I don't know why. You just surprised me is all … and I wasn't sure how to react. To be honest, I thought maybe you were some sort of sea creature. A goddess of the night…"

"Goddess of the night, eh? That's a little dramatic." Kathi Jo slipped off her flip-flops and took one step toward the water.

I blushed. "I'm a writer. I guess my imagination runs away with me sometimes."

Instead of moving on to another subject or teasing me about writing, Kathi Jo raised her eyebrows with interest.

"A writer? That's pretty amazing."

"Do you write, too?"

Kathi Jo shook her head. "No, but I like to read. Maybe I can read your stories one day." She stretched one foot out, making a slow rippled circle in the water.

"So you like to read, and you like to go swimming naked at midnight," I chaffed, lowering myself to the edge of the water beside her.

"Yes. Why not?" she said, giddily.

For a few moments everything was quiet, just two strangers with our feet in the water, cooking under the summer sun. I had so many questions. How old was she? How did she feel about living in this tiny lake town year-round? Why did they move here from the other side of the lake? And where did she get that tattoo and those strange piercings?

I was trying to decide which to ask first, when Kathi Jo leaned in close, shadows dancing in the hollows of her cheeks. Her lips brushed against my ear.

"Want to see a dead body?" she whispered.

Chapter Two

CAN YOU KEEP A SECRET?

CURRENT DAY

The lake house was like stepping through the Looking Glass with Alice in that old children's tale everything hazy and distorted. Of course, I'd been inside since returning to town, but now things were … different.

The dead animals on the walls had been taken down by Cindy and the rest of the crew. The old-timey red drapes that clashed with the lime green paint were gone; bundled up in a corner of the room, like a bloody tumor. I stood in the doorway, Cindy breathing down my neck, unable to force my legs to move closer to the bedroom.

When I found out the lake house was mine, it couldn't have come at a better time. Jason was the breadwinner in our marriage, his salary as a principal dwarfing my meager part-time earnings from teaching; so, when I filed for divorce, there was no doubt that I would be the one leaving. I couldn't afford the mortgage on our 300K house; I could barely afford the cheap apartment I was renting across the lake while I waited on these renovations to finish up.

But my inheritance from my parents offered me a new solution: I could either sell the lake house for a decent profit—houses here were worth much more than they used to be when my parents were my age now—or I could keep it as a rental property, using the money as an extra source of steady income while I figured out what to do about teaching and where to live.

There was a third option: staying in Hillendale, keeping the house for myself. But I certainly didn't want to do that. There were good memories here, but also ugly ones.

Hillendale, albeit a small town, was a great investment these days, according to my realtor. People rented out houses and cottages here every summer, some of them for upward of $500–1,000 per night. City people with money were dying for a slice of the "rugged" life, nestled in this small Kentucky lakeside town. Although the houses here weren't at all what I would consider "rugged".

I'd allowed the realtor to pressure me a bit, finally

taking out a home improvement loan to do the repairs on the lake house. *If you're going to rent it out, or even sell it, you need to do it right. Maximize your profits,* the realtor had explained. She was right about the house needing improvements: it had sat empty for years, our days of family visits and vacations long gone.

The whole house had that unused smell about it— damp and musty, like the inside of a sealed-up tomb. It needed a lot of work, inside and out. Landscaping, concrete patio repairs, gutters, carpet…

More work than I'd initially expected.

Most of my visits had been short and sweet, checking on the state of repairs and collaborating with the company I'd hired to do the job. The past few weeks, their work has mostly been done on the exterior.

But tonight, here I was … stepping inside it, moving back through time…

The house was a maze—scaffolding in the living room, buckets of unopened paint, tools, and ladders clogging up every open space and pathway.

I forced myself onward, putting one foot in front of the other, snaking around the crew's equipment.

"It's in there," Cindy said, her voice raw like she'd just been screaming. I flinched at the sound of it; I'd nearly forgotten she was behind me.

"Which room?"

She pointed down the long dark hallway that led to

the main bedroom, the one my parents slept in every summer when we came to the lake.

"Wait." I turned around to look at Cindy. In the low-lit living room, I could see her face, the pallor of her skin almost green. As I stepped closer to her, I caught a whiff of something sour, perhaps vomit on her clothes.

"What were you doing here this late, Cindy?" It was an important question, but nothing that couldn't have waited until after I looked at what was in that bedroom. But I needed to know; her late-night presence here was not only unusual, but it was also unnerving and unprofessional.

Cindy stammered, "I-I..."

"It's okay. I just want to know why."

Cindy lowered her eyes. "I had a row with my husband. A bad one, worse than usual. I live over in Greenville, you know?"

I nodded, although I wasn't as familiar with Hillendale or its neighboring towns as I should have been. Greenville wasn't far, I did know that; just a short commute for her to the site each day.

"I didn't know where else to go, and I tend to focus on my work when I'm upset. I love breaking shit when I'm pissed."

"Breaking shit?"

"Yeah, that's why I brought my sledgehammer. We're

going to knock down the wall between the master and the spare, create a walk-in closet, yeah?" Cindy said.

"Yeah." My head was spinning. I couldn't remember all that was on the agenda; and with whatever was going on now, none of it probably mattered anymore.

"I started smashing and it felt good. I figured the guys wouldn't mind me getting an early start … but then I stopped for a smoke break. And…"

"And?"

"And while I was smoking, I took a look around the rooms. I wanted to size them up, get a feel for what it would look like when we were done. That's when I opened the closet," Cindy said.

With that, there was no more time for stalling. Slowly, I entered the hallway, eyes focused on the room at its very end.

The door was open, the room casting an orange, ghostly glow from within. For a moment, I could almost imagine my parents in there: Dad on the left side of the bed with his reading glasses, working a crossword; Mom on the right, buffing her nails, hair twisted up in rollers as part of her nighttime routine.

But when I stepped inside there was nothing, just an empty room. The bed and the nightstands were gone. My parents were gone. And the door to the bedroom closet was open.

"Did you call the police?" I asked Cindy, breathlessly, frozen six feet away from the closet.

"No. I wanted to call you first."

It seemed like a strange reaction, but I was grateful she had called me. I had to see this for myself. Had to see if it was real.

As I approached the closet, I could sense that Cindy was no longer behind me. When I glanced back, she was hovering in the doorway, bracing her hands on the frame.

I took a breath and stepped closer. There was no lighting in the closet. A memory came out of nowhere: Mom bitching that Dad was too lazy to install a light fixture and she had to reach in blind for her clothes. That was around the time the fighting started…

All of Mom's summer clothes were gone now—the shirts and shorts, the flimsy summer dresses, and jumpers… All that remained was a long metal bar and a handful of dingy wire hangers.

And the long black dress bag on the floor of the closet.

I knew without opening it that that was where the body laid. The bag obviously contained something solid, the sides bulging. The shape of shoulders and … and a head.

"You zipped it back up after?" I said, flabbergasted, looking back at Cindy.

"Yeah. I couldn't... I didn't want to see those eyes anymore." Her voice shook.

Squatting down on my haunches, I reached for the slim black zipper at the top of the bag.

"Wait. Maybe we shouldn't touch it anymore... Maybe we should call and wait for someone to..."

But it was too late to go back now. I couldn't wait another second. I had to see whose body was inside that bag.

Cindy made a strange gurgling noise as I tugged the zipper all the way down, exposing the secrets within.

SUMMER OF '98

"Can you keep a secret?" Kathi Jo asked.

We had borrowed her mother's banana yellow kayak. Although I'd offered to take a turn, Kathi Jo held tightly to the oars, rowing farther and farther from the bank. Our houses grew smaller and smaller as she rowed us further into the lake.

I was surprised my mom had agreed to it; I was only thirteen and she never let me swim in the water without her keeping a watchful eye. But Kathi Jo's mother had jumped in with a "yes" before my mother could respond, and as it turned out, Kathi Jo was a year older than me; she was fourteen. *She's an excellent swimmer. I'm sure they won't go far,* Isabella had reassured my mother, for which I was grateful.

"I can keep a secret," I said. Scooting forward on the hard yellow seat, we were so close our knees were touching.

Kathi Jo had mentioned a body. That had to be some sort of joke, right?

"I found bones in the basement when we moved in, in this tiny little nook in the wall. At first, I thought they were plastic, some sort of Halloween shit left behind. But then … I touched them. They weren't props, that's for sure. Something terrible happened in that house," Kathi Jo said.

A chill ran from the base of my neck all the way down the length of my spine. My family had vacationed here every summer since I could remember—how many times had I played close to the house next door? I'd never gone inside it. But there were times when I'd been afraid that someone was in there, looking out the windows, watching when it was supposed to be empty…

"What kind of bones?" I asked.

Kathi Jo held the oar steady. I stared at the chipped black polish on her nails.

"Some of them could be animal bones. It's hard to know for certain. But one of them is clearly a jawbone … I'm starting to think maybe it's a full body, the skeleton in pieces…"

So, that's what she meant by wanting to see a "body".

"What did your mom say about it?"

Kathi Jo shook her head solemnly. "I didn't tell her."

"What! Why?" Sometimes I couldn't stand my mom and dad, but if I found a body—or bones—in the house, I sure as shit would run screaming for them.

"I knew she'd call the cops and then they'd take them. Or worse, they'd take our whole house. Mom just bought this place. I don't want to move again ... not after all the stuff with my dad..." Kathi Jo said.

Kathi Jo stopped rowing and bit her lip. It was a nervous tic that over time, I'd come to recognize and find endearing.

Two things struck me then about Kathi Jo: she hadn't had an easy life, and she was the bravest person I knew. I couldn't imagine finding random bones in my new basement and keeping that all to myself.

"So, what are you going to do?" I asked. It came out louder than I'd intended, my voice echoing across the fog-covered lake, bouncing back and forth through the trees. I prayed our mothers weren't sitting out back, overhearing everything. Sound really travels on water.

"Not me. *Us.* Now that you know the secret, what are we going to do? How are we going to solve this?" Kathi Jo asked.

Chapter Three

SCENE OF THE CRIME

CURRENT DAY

Have you ever done something you couldn't take back? Wished so hard you could reel it back in, swallow it down, forget the whole thing ever happened? And worse ... have you ever seen something you couldn't unsee? Something that burns on the back of your eyelids and haunts you every time you close your eyes?

Well, that's what this is—a dividing line. A before and after. There was the version of me that existed before I opened that bag, and she's been replaced with the girl who can't unsee the dead body of her childhood friend. *Best friend.*

My body rocked with revulsion, sending me scurrying across the room like a backwards crab, the back of my head connecting with the wall behind me. In an instant, Cindy was at my side, putting hands on both of my shoulders.

"Please don't touch me!" I screamed. I leaned forward on my knees, pushing myself off the floor until I was back on my feet. This time, I took a deeper breath and tried to prepare myself.

"Hold up your phone torch, will ya? The light in here is shit," I said.

Cindy fumbled for her phone, finally lifting it, shakily, aiming for the open door to the closet. Together, we walked back toward the plastic bag. In that moment, I wished I were anywhere but here … *Take me back to the trailer in Branton or that awful house with my ex, I don't care. I'll go anywhere besides this house, this room, this closet … I don't want to see it again.*

"Aim it down for me, straight at her," I said, shakily, sinking slowly to my knees beside the bag.

The torch flickered off the walls of the cavernous closet, settling on the top end of the bag.

There was a smell, but nothing like I would have imagined—it only smelled damp. Moldy. Like dead insects and spoiled garbage. Nothing like you'd imagine a body would smell like.

Two eyes, milky white, stared back at me through a

sheaf of plastic. I covered my mouth with my hand, stifling a scream.

The body inside the bag was like a mummy, tightly wound in some sort of plastic saran wrap. The skin stretched taut over bone. The lips, like two dark earthworms, were slightly parted. And a piercing—the kind of signature piercing you just can't miss.

It had been nearly two decades since I'd seen my friend, but I had no doubt—the body in the closet belonged to Kathi Jo Redfield.

SUMMER OF '98

To make a long story short, there were no human bones in Kathi Jo's basement that summer. But, when I arrived at her house for our sleepover, and she took me down there to see the "bones", I wasn't a bit disappointed. In fact, I was hugely relieved.

They were a pile of old chicken bones and a hollowed-out turkey carcass, probably left behind by some careless young renters and picked over by furry scavengers during the cold season.

"You're not mad at me for lying, are ya?" Kathi Jo asked.

I could see the nervous look in her eyes; she was waiting for me to react.

I shrugged. "They look like real bones to me. Definitely a body," I said.

Kathi Jo smiled.

"Okay, good. Now, let's lay the bones out so we can begin our analysis. You brought the notebook, right? Do you mind taking down the case details?" She was stooped over the "dead body", a too-large baseball cap tucked down low over her brow, and I was seated in a hard metal chair we'd found in the corner of the unfinished basement, covered in cobwebs and dust.

All day, the build-up to our sleepover—my first ever sleepover, in fact—had been unbearable. I'd felt a mixture of excitement and fear about our plans for the night ahead.

But now that I was here, and I realized it was all a game, all I could feel were jitters of exhilaration coursing through my veins. Apparently, I wasn't the only one with a big imagination. Kathi Jo liked to make up stories too.

Somehow, I knew in that very moment, that Kathi Jo and I were destined to be best friends.

For the next few hours, we picked that basement apart. Kathi Jo found what looked like a partial footprint, left behind in the dusty old earth near the bone nook. Together, we gathered supplies—scotch tape, a disposable camera with a few pictures left in it, and a long wooden yardstick. We tried to make a mold of the print, and we used the tape all around the basement, trying to find full or partial fingerprints of the killer.

I took notes, short and succinct, while she did most of the legwork.

"I don't want to sound sexist, but I think this shoe print definitely belongs to a female. Size five, five and a half maybe?" Kathi Jo dictated, while I scribbled faster on my notepad. I was fairly certain that the shoeprint belonged to one of us, but I just kept going with it.

I paused, chewing on the end of my pencil. "Or possibly a child. Even a teen?"

Kathi Jo stood. "You might be right, Watson."

"Watson?" I said, perplexed.

"Never mind," she waved me away. "I think this was a good day's work, Willow. We are this much closer to catching the killer and hopefully identifying our poor victim."

Kathi Jo sounded so serious, and I was totally here for it. As much as I hated to admit it, summers at Hillendale were lonely. Sure, I had my parents and, sometimes, there were other kids out with their parents on the lake that I talked to or played with. But they rarely stayed past the weekend.

Let's face it, I was well past the age of role-playing and make-believe. At least I'd thought I was—until Kathi Jo came along.

"I'm tired," Kathi Jo said, tossing the ball cap aside and wiping sweat from her brow. The basement was thick with heat and dust, not enough air in the space to go around.

"Okay. We can go to bed if you want to," I said, trying to hide my disappointment. It's not that I wasn't tired too; I hadn't been awake past one in the morning in a long time … but I hated for the sleepover to end. Playing detectives with Kathi Jo was fun. And, somehow, I didn't feel silly or childish doing it. I felt like we were on the same wavelength. Watson and… I couldn't remember the other guy's name.

"No way! I said I was tired, not ready for bed, silly. Let's go for a swim," Kathi Jo said.

My cheeks warmed. As much fun as I was having, I didn't want to go skinny dipping with my newly made friend. Or with anyone, for that matter. I wasn't long and lithe like Kathi Jo; my body was short and pudgy, and I always felt too big and wrinkled in my own strange skin.

Kathi Jo offered her hand, and I took it. She tugged me to my feet, and I brushed the basement dust and debris off my jeans.

"We have to be quiet though. My mom's usually a heavy sleeper, but you never know. Being in a new place, I never know what I can get away with," Kathi Jo said.

Her words made me wonder for the first time: how

much trouble is this girl? What sort of things has she gotten away with in the past?

"Okay. I'll be quiet," I said, words like whispers as we climbed the dark wooden staircase, emerging out of the basement and into Kathi Jo's low-lit kitchen. There was a silly clock on the wall, the tail of a big black cat swooshing side to side.

Kathi Jo's house was larger than ours. It felt homier, too—no dead animals or dirty old furniture; it was sparsely decorated, but the furniture was cute and modern. There were photographs in expensive-looking frames on the mantel and walls; a couple of half-burned candles and bunches of incense scattered around. A handwoven blanket slung across the loveseat. I loved it, the whole vibe...

There was a part of me that felt jealous of Kathi Jo's family situation, too. The fact that Kathi Jo had her mother all to herself and got to live in vacationland all year long ... it didn't feel fair.

The screen door was unlocked. Kathi Jo held it open for me, breathlessly, and I slid through. She slithered out behind me, skinny as a snake through the crack, silently closing the back door behind us.

"What are we going to do?" I whispered, as we tiptoed toward the woods. I stole a glance over at my parents' house. In my mind, I'd hoped my parents would make a night of it, with me being gone and all. Perhaps stay up late, do something romantic. But they weren't the romantic type. And I was half convinced that they were only together because of their shared interest in me. The house was dark, all the lights out. They'd probably gone to bed early, or Dad was getting drunk in the dark by himself the way he did some nights.

Kathi Jo held a finger to her lips and pointed. The yellow kayak glowed softly in the light of the moon, still resting on the edge of the bank where we'd had it earlier.

Thoughts of having to undress wormed through my brain. I thought about that Meatloaf song that came out a few years ago—*I would do anything for love, but I won't do that.*

I wasn't in love with Kathi Jo, but I'd started to love the possibility of our budding friendship. However, I wasn't taking off my clothes for anyone. *I won't do that.*

My body was a bag of nerves as I climbed in the boat, knees shaking and boat rocking side-to-side. I was a decent swimmer; still, falling out of the boat in the daytime was one thing. Tumbling over into deep water in the dark...? *No, thank you.*

Kathi Jo climbed in next, holding the oar in front of her like a dazzling shield.

"What are we going to do out here?" I asked, breathily.

"I heard there's an iceberg out there somewhere. But

luckily, we have a ship that cannot sink. The best ship ever built," Kathi Jo said in a deep, stern voice, patting the side of the plastic boat.

I couldn't help it; my mouth spread into a shit-eating grin. "You've seen *Titanic*?!"

The blockbuster movie had released last year, and I'd gone to see it in the theaters twice. The first time was with Jenny Buckworth, a sort-of friend; our mothers liked to arrange awkward "playdates" between us, like we were still in diapers or something. But the movie plan worked out perfectly; in fact, I'd barely remembered that Jenny was there as I scarfed down a bucket of popcorn and a box of bitter Snowcaps, gasping at some scenes, while bawling through others.

Instantly, I'd fallen in love with Jack and Rose.

"The movie was all right," Jenny had sniffed, sliding in the back of her mother's van after the movie let out.

Just all right?! I was obsessed! That's when I knew Jenny and I weren't going to be friends.

A month later, after much cajoling, I convinced my mom to take me again. Luckily, she seemed to enjoy it more than that bore Jenny, but she practically turned green during the scene where Jack draws Rose's tits, then bangs her in the back of that cool old Coupé de Ville.

Kathi Jo cleared her throat, bringing me back to reality. "Titanic, you say? So, you have heard the name of my unsinkable ship! Will you sail with me then, taking a leap of faith?"

That was another thing I learned about Kathi Jo—she never broke character. We were a lot alike, in that way.

"Of course, I will. If you jump, I jump, Jack," I said, taking the oar in my hands.

Chapter Four

THE MORE THINGS CHANGE, THE MORE THEY STAY THE SAME

CURRENT DAY

There was nothing else I could do at the house. As soon as the police arrived, they cast Cindy and me aside as though we were trespassers.

In a tiny town in the middle of nowhere, you might assume it would take hours to find enough police officers to work a murder scene. But perhaps the town being slow and small was precisely the reason *everyone* turned out to see the body.

The normally quiet street in front of the lake house, with its few lonely neighbors that only visited once a year, was crammed with police cars. Even an ambulance and a fire truck came.

"Jeez, we called the cops, not the whole fucking

village," Cindy murmured, steering me toward the passenger's side of her clunky blue Saab. She'd insisted on driving me back home, an unnecessarily long trip around the lake, even though it only took a few minutes to jog through the woods and go across, using rickety Holman's Bridge.

"I can walk, seriously. I'll probably have to come right back over in a few hours anyway, when the police finish with the crime scene," I said.

Cindy climbed behind the wheel, nodding insistently for me to get in. "Shall I remind you that we just found a woman's body? No way am I letting you walk through those woods alone."

"She's not just any woman, and she's less woman and more girl..." I took a seat, falling back on the headrest with a sigh, and tugged the door shut for privacy. I'd known a couple of the police officers; they'd been kids back then, when Kathi Jo went missing. The thought of all of them in there with her, instead of me, made my stomach sick and swirly. But, also, I never wanted to go in that room again either...

"I heard you telling the cops that you knew her. And I saw the look of shock on your face when you opened that bag," Cindy said. I could feel her studying the side of my face, begging me to indulge her curiosity.

"Well, I think finding a dead body in your closet would give anyone a scare."

"Yeah, but your face ... I can't even describe it. It was like you knew. You knew..." Cindy said.

"You're right. I knew it was Kathi Jo," I said, sullenly. "The moment you told me ... I knew it had to be her. Nobody else has ever gone missing from Hillendale ... not that I know of. But all this time she wasn't missing like we all thought... She was dead," I choked out the words. I still couldn't believe it. After all this time ... it made no sense. Why would her body turn up now? And who put it there? My thoughts whirled out of control.

"I've heard about Kathi Jo Redfield. But that was before my time. Can you tell me what happened?" Cindy pressed.

I shook my head back and forth, staring out the passenger window. I tried to catch a glimpse through the curtains; tried to see what they were doing inside the lake house, what more they had discovered.

"She went missing a long time ago. When we were kids," I explained.

"How do you know it was her and not someone else? It could be anyone in that bag."

"I'm sure, Cindy," I said, flatly. Those eyes, that ice-white freckly skin ... her piercing. The short, raven hair. All of it gave her away. *But how did her body stay so fresh ... so pristine? And her hair wasn't threaded with gray like mine; no wrinkles on her skin ... Kathi Jo hadn't aged. Which means … which means she died all those years ago, and everyone back then was wrong. Including me.*

"Were you really close?" Cindy asked.

I gave a weary sigh. Her questions were not only probing; they felt ridiculous and insensitive. But when I looked over at Cindy's face, open and worrisome, I could tell it wasn't just morbid curiosity fueling her questions. She seemed concerned for me. *She really cares,* I thought.

"Sorry. I didn't mean to ask so many questions… It's not every day you see something like this, not in a town like this one…" Cindy said.

"Yeah, we were friends. We spent time together when I came here on vacation… She lived in the house next door," I explained.

"Next door to the lake house? Are you serious? I didn't see any other houses close to it…" Cindy seemed youthful again, her over-eager questions making me feel ill at ease and tired.

"Sorry. I mean, the house that used to be there. I think they tore it down a few years ago. Someone bought the land, but they haven't built anything on it yet." I spoke. Turning my head, I squinted at the empty field of grass beside the lake house, the place that used to hold so much memory, so many secrets…

All gone now. Just like Kathi Jo.

"What do you think happened to her?" Cindy

reached for her seatbelt. I jumped at the loud click as she snapped it over her chest.

"I used to think … well, I always hoped that she had just run off. That she was out there somewhere, living a better life. Away from me and this town … but I was wrong. All along I was wrong."

"She never left," Cindy said, her words so low I could barely register them.

"She never left," I repeated, the words painful in my chest. "I was the last one to see her that summer night, and she was angry and troubled when we parted ways. It wasn't until the next morning that her mom found the note—a simple goodbye and no explanation for why she was leaving. But it wasn't all that surprising, not really. Her mom and dad had split up, and Kathi Jo had been distancing herself from her family for a while before she left." Now I was recalling that night, all the details … less for Cindy's benefit and more for my own. How long had it been since I'd let it all play out in my mind … since I'd relived those final moments with my friend?

"I'm really sorry about your friend," Cindy said, softly.

I looked across the grass just as the front door of the lake house snapped open. A detective ran down the porch steps and came around the side of the house. I thought I could hear the sounds of his retching from here.

"Kathi Jo…" I muttered her name aloud, to no one in particular.

I couldn't believe it. After all this time, the truth was finally here. At least partly.

Kathi Jo never left Lake Hillendale. She didn't run away at all, which was what the police, her family, and townspeople had all assumed.

She never went anywhere at all. All along she had been right here, rotting in the place where our friendship began…

SUMMER OF '99

"What do you think will happen when the clock strikes twelve?" Kathi Jo asked me, her face deadpan and serious.

We were talking about Y2K; everyone was. When the new year rolled over and it became 2000, shit was going to hit the fan. All because of some stupid computer error, according to my mom and dad.

"I don't know," I said, rolling onto my back on Kathi Jo's bed. I lifted the joint to my lips and took a small enough puff, one that wouldn't leave me choking and gagging this time.

"Blow that shit out the window, will ya? Mom will be home soon," Kathi Jo warned. I rolled my eyes, but I sat up on my elbows, and sent my next tiny curl of smoke out the port hole opening that was considered a window.

A lot had changed since I last saw Kathi Jo; but also, things had stayed the same. When my family left Hillendale at the end of August, I'd hidden under a blanket in the backseat for the whole ride home, unsuccessfully trying to hold back tears. I hadn't wanted to go back to Branton. To that stupid trailer park with my stupid "friends", to the school I was dreading...

That first summer, meeting Kathi Jo, had been the best of my life and I wasn't ready to leave her. Back to my old life ... riding bikes in the trailer park with the neighborhood kids, Parker Valley middle school, endless hours of boredom and homework...

The first couple weeks back were the hardest. I missed swimming with Kathi Jo. I missed sitting beside her and writing my stories, while she read hers. Most of all, I missed our late-night adventures, playing make-believe and talking about our would-be futures.

Kathi Jo wanted to be a Hollywood actress. *Serious roles*, she said. *Like the one Rose played in* Titanic.

After school settled in in Branton, and I got back in the swing of things with my friends and my schedule, I'd felt better. Kathi Jo had finally downloaded AOL Instant Messenger so we could chat any time we wanted when we were both online.

She told me about her school—*who knew that Hillendale had a school?! Not me!*

She even told me about a few local boys she'd met and wanted to introduce me to in the summer. I'd wondered a few times if they, like the rest of her stories, were only make-believe.

And tonight, my second day back at the lake house,, I was finally going to find out.

"So, what's the plan for tonight?" I asked.

Kathi Jo had promised to introduce me to the guys. But, in truth, I held on to hope that maybe tonight would be just about us. Perhaps we could watch *Titanic*—the DVD would be out later this summer, but I'd picked up the boxy VHS set, on sale at Hollywood Video.

"Well, Blake is working at Cluck's till eleven. So, we won't be able to sneak out and see them until after that. Mom should be home by ten. She usually passes out by eleven or twelve," Kathi Jo said, reaching for the joint.

She had started smoking some this year, spilling her secret over AIM during one of our late-night talks. I'd been shaken by it, honestly. There were kids at my school who smoked weed, obviously, but none that I hung out with regularly. However, I'd sort of bent the truth ... telling her I'd tried pot too.

Lying to my best friend felt wrong, but now it wasn't a lie anymore. I'd been smoking with Kathi Jo every night since arriving back at the lake last week.

I'd been afraid at first; the thought of giving up control, unsure how my body would react to the drug, was frightening. But disappointing my best friend was even scarier—despite our long talks through the fall and winter, I'd felt strangely distant from her, like each day we were both changing into different people.

At night, when I was alone with my thoughts and unable to sleep, I'd often closed my eyes and allowed my mind to drift all the way across the state ... all the way back to Lake Hillendale. I liked to imagine what the house looked like and felt like when my family and I weren't occupying it. And I liked to imagine Kathi Jo, sulking in her mother's home, watching the darkened windows of the lake house next door, wishing I were there to keep her company.

"So, this Blake ... is he your boyfriend, then?" I asked.

Despite all of our online conversations, she had never clarified their status, which seemed pretty important these days.

"Not officially." Kathi Jo wet her thumb and point finger, pinching the tip of the joint to extinguish the fire.

"What does that mean, exactly?"

Kathi Jo shrugged. "It means what it means, I guess. I try not to worry about it too much." Her eyes were skinny slits; she had smoked way more of the joint than I had.

I had to wonder if it was Blake that had turned her on

to the weed. I could remember her, just last summer, bitching about the sour smell of her mom's cigarettes and how they left behind an odor on her clothes.

"What did you say his friend's name was?" My eyes travelled the circumference of Kathi Jo's room. It was still the same as last summer, but a few things had changed. She'd replaced her Luke Perry posters with Kurt Cobain and a few other singers I didn't recognize. She was a year older than me, but still. Our interests were mostly the same. *Except the pot and the boys.*

She was growing up, I suppose. I was too. Although, there hadn't been any guys I'd been interested in at school—not really. I'd mostly hung around the same group of girls I always had, a mixture of preps and nerds, and I'd spent a lot of time thinking about the summer. Thinking about getting back to the lake with Kathi Jo.

But she'd been busy, running around the lake with Blake and his friends. I couldn't help feeling green about it, wishing it were me she was hanging around with during the school year instead of them.

"He has two friends, Tommy and Trevor. I think they're both equally cute. Not as cute as my Blake though, of course…" Kathi Jo said.

I crossed my legs, criss cross applesauce we used to call it. I tried my best to act interested.

"So, tell me about Blake. Is he a good kisser?" I asked.

At this, Kathi Jo flashed a mischievous smile, showing

me all her teeth. "He's the best kisser, ever. And we've done other things…"

Alarmed by these "other things", I opened my mouth to ask questions, but was quickly shushed by Kathi Jo when the front door slammed shut downstairs.

"Kat! I'm home!" Isabella Redfield sounded just the same—tired and leery. As a single mom, she worked long hours as an accountant.

Kathi Jo went to her bedroom door and stuck her head out. "Hey, Mom! Willow's back in town. She's staying the night. Is that okay?"

"Sure, sweetheart. You girls don't stay up too late tonight though, all right? I don't want you getting too far off your school schedules…"

Kathi Jo looked over at me and rolled her eyes. She wedged the door to her bedroom shut and returned to the bed. Getting off our sleep schedules should have been the least of our parents' worries.

I glanced at my Adidas wristband—still a couple of hours until we had to go meet the boys.

"What should we do till then?" I asked, tapping my watch.

I'd hoped it would be like last summer, magic and mayhem … but instead, it was another "M"—make-up.

"We need all the time we can get to fix up. I got my crimper warming up. Let's dress to impress!" Kathi Jo squealed. The make-up was new; something she must have bought over the winter and fall. Back home in Branton, I only owned a few lip glosses and a tube of mascara I didn't use.

I leaned back on the bed, watching her open and unload her caboodle, spreading cosmetics over the bed. She looked so excited about it, and I wanted to feel that too.

Kathi Jo was still the same, but also different.

Chapter Five

INTRODUCTIONS

CURRENT DAY

We rode in silence for the first half of the short journey. But, with Cindy, silence never seemed to last long.

"You're staying at the bait shop, right?" Cindy was smoking, her window cracked, and her voice sounded like a pack-a-day habit. Usually, the smoke smell would have bothered me, but I was mostly oblivious, my body humming with ... what? Fear or anxiety? I wasn't sure. Perhaps it was sadness, my body still unable to accept the fact that Kathi Jo was really gone.

Not just gone ... murdered.

No one with good intentions wraps a body in plastic, then stuffs it in a long black bag.

But ... it doesn't seem like they went to any real effort to hide it either. Whoever put the body there must have known it would be discovered, workers at the house every day...

Nothing about this made sense to me. I'd lost her all those years ago, and part of me had accepted it over the years. But I didn't expect this ... not to find her that way, and not after all this time.

My eyes stung with tears.

Beside me, Cindy was still talking.

"Bait shop, right?" she repeated.

I swiped furiously at my cheeks. "Sorry. Yes. It's not the bait shop, really. It's closed down for the season. I'm just renting out the room above," I said, absently.

The parking lot in front of Bart's Baits was empty, as usual. One lonely streetlamp created ghoulish shadows on the darkened street.

Luckily, I'd left a couple of lights on in my upstairs apartment—one bonus of leaving in such a hurry. Taking the rickety metal stairs to the upper apartment was scary enough without having to do it in total darkness. Tonight, I was thankful for the interior lights and Cindy's company.

Cindy unhooked her belt and looked over at me, leerily. "You okay?"

I nodded. Suddenly, I remembered our conversation from earlier ... her reason for being alone at the "job site" late at night.

"You said you were fighting with your husband. Do you want to come up? Stay here for a bit?" I barely knew this woman, but I could understand the fear and discomfort of returning home to an angry spouse. I wondered if their fight was a simple row, or something far worse. I knew a little too much about what that was like, too...

"Thanks, but I think I'll head home. Dealing with Bruce right now sounds better than sticking around here with a murderer on the loose ... no offense," Cindy said.

I winced. "None taken," I lied. I was tempted to explain to her that it wasn't *my* town either... I was transient, only staying for as long as I had to until the work was done.

The work ... none of it even matters now, I realized. *Who's going to rent or buy a house where a dead body was found?*

Why am I so worried about money right now? A girl is dead. And not just any girl ... Kathi Jo, I reminded myself.

I shook my head back and forth, a feeble attempt at banishing from my mind that waxy look in her eyes, her skin slick beneath a sheen of heavy plastic... *How did she die? What did they do to her?* I couldn't shake off the rapid thoughts and growing turmoil inside me.

There was a time when we were thick as thieves. A time when I would have done anything for Kathi Jo, but those summers felt so long ago, tipping on the edges of my memories.

"Well, thank you for the ride," I said, a lump in my throat. "Drive safe back to Greenville. I'll update you and the crew at some point tomorrow or the next day if I can, let you know what our next move is."

Cindy grimaced. "Okay, sounds good. I'll watch you till you get in. Make sure you're safe." She pointed at the bait shop.

"Thanks again," I said, closing the car door softly behind me.

The metal stairwell clunked and moaned as I climbed to my second-floor apartment. I'd got it for a good deal and hadn't had to sign a lease. Four hundred and fifty bucks a month was perfect for my dwindling budget. But the shop below was dark and haunting, the isolated apartment on top cramped and lonely at night. And the whole apartment smelled like oil and fish, no matter how much deodorizer I sprayed or how many candles I lit.

I dug around in my bag, reaching for my keys. When I reached the top creaky stair, I gave a little wave down to Cindy.

As she backed out of the parking lot, I realized I didn't need my keys anyway—I'd left the door unlocked, rushing down the steps and cutting through the woods in a hurry after the call came in.

I closed the heavy door behind me, locking it tight.

Something soft brushed against my ankle. My fat tabby, Smokey, gave me a disapproving meow. She'd come with the place; apparently, this space belonged to her before it did me. I'd never owned a cat before, and had no interest in it, but she'd grown on me, curling up beside me on the lumpy twin mattress, doing a funny little ritual with her paws on the couch cushions before she climbed up beside me.

"Oh, Smokey. I missed you, girl." I scooped her up in my arms, heavy as she was, and carried her into the kitchen.

Smokey would let me pick her up from time to time, usually when she missed me, but she couldn't tolerate me for too long. She started struggling in my arms, and I released her on the old scratchy wood floors before one of her back claws tore my skin.

The apartment was tiny; the rooms bleeding into one another like a gelatinous blob. Living room and dining room were together, a miniature galley kitchen, and then a small bedroom with a cramped bathroom attached. The washroom was so small, I had to suck in my gut to get the door closed between the wall and the commode.

The lighting in the whole place was poor. After moving in, I'd bought a couple of lamps, one for my bedroom, and another for the living room area. There were no fans, only a dusty old box fan in the closet that I hadn't pulled out yet. And the smell. I wasn't sure if it was in my head, or remnants from the fish store below, but I couldn't shake the feeling that it was permeating everything, my clothes and hair. Even my food. *Yuck.*

I forced myself through the motions: opening a can of Fancy Feast for Smokey, checking on her water bowl and litter box. It hadn't sunk in yet, the reality of what I was facing.

A dead body in my newly inherited lake house. And not just any body—the missing remains of Kathi Jo. After all this time, there she was. Wrapped up like a piece of deli meat, stowed away like last week's trash. It wasn't right. Regardless of the past, Kathi Jo didn't deserve that. Nobody does.

I sat down at the flimsy kitchen table, listening to the sound of Smokey slurping salmon juice from her bowl.

If Kathi Jo were here right now ... if this were one of our role-playing games ... we'd be laying out the facts, analyzing things piece by piece.

I opened my notebook and scratched out a few things I knew:

Kathi Jo has been missing for a long time. She left a note. Everyone believed she had run away, even me.

If someone killed her—and they obviously did—how did her body stay so pristine? There was no smell, not really...

Did the body look older? Like someone had held her for a while? No. That haircut and those piercings ... it looked like the body of a teenage girl. The same teen girl who went missing.

Who killed her and why?

How did her body end up at <u>my</u> lake house? She hasn't been there all this time ... the house was thoroughly cleaned less than a few months before construction began.

The search party for Kathi Jo combed the entire neighborhood and lake, even though the assumption was that she ran away. If no one found her body at the time, then ... where has it been all these years?

Someone placed her inside my lake house. WHY?! WHO?!

WHY my place? Why ME? Is this some sort of message? And if so, what could the message be?

I thought I was the last to see her alive before she left town, but now I know that I was wrong...

This list is pointless.

I was about to crumple up the paper and throw it, when someone banged on the door of my apartment. I jumped out of the chair—out of my skin, really—and stared at the closed tan door to my apartment. I hadn't heard a car pull in. *Did Cindy change her mind and come back?* Or perhaps the police wanted to speak with me ... they'd practically blown off both Cindy and me when they arrived, insisting we clear the area immediately.

As I walked toward the door, someone knocked again. Softer this time.

"Willow, it's me. Can we talk?" A man's voice coming through the door.

I drew in a deep breath, then let it out slowly. It had been years since I'd heard his voice, but I knew who it was instantly. I unchained the deadbolt, slid the lock over, and opened the door. I welcomed Tommy inside.

SUMMER '99

Houses in Hillendale were mostly the same. Worn down, but well loved. Single family homes with overgrown yards lined Albertson Avenue as Kathi Jo and I walked, arms intertwined and a hop in our step due to the heady floating feel of the pot we'd smoked on the way over.

Even though it was well past midnight, there were people awake in Hillendale. Mostly the out-of-towners, like my family: people renting out houses or staying with friends. Lazy towels were draped over clothes lines and picnic tables, the smell of sunscreen, fishing tackle, bug repellant, and bonfires clinging to the sticky night air.

I wondered what it was like to live here in the fall, or even the winter. How barren the place must feel; how nice it would feel to take ownership of it all.

"You look hot, ya know." Kathi Jo poked me in the ribs with her elbow and leaned her head to the side, smiling. "Aren't you glad you let me do your make-up?"

I was glad.

I felt pretty, beautiful even. My eyes were kohl-rimmed with soft gray shadow. She'd painted my nails sparkly pink and coated my sunburned arms and chest with this cold, sticky body glitter that came in a tube. My whole body sparkled in the moonlight; a sense of magic in the air all around me. *Was it just the pot and the cheap ass wine cooler I'd drunk, or did the world seem realer—more sharply in focus—than ever before?*

"You look pretty, too," I said. And she did. Kathi Jo wore a black and grey plaid skirt with thin, sexy leggings and a white baby tee. Apparently, the naughty schoolgirl look was in style—who knew? They forced us to wear school uniforms at Parker Valley, so wearing something like that in my leisure time wasn't my thing.

Kathi Jo had offered me a few of her baby doll dresses, but I'd settled on a cute camisole, my acid-washed jeans, and sneakers. The jeans were loose around the waist, hiding all my fatal flaws.

As I followed Kathi Jo along the semi-familiar roads I'd rode down in the car with my family, I felt my nerves coming back. *Who were these boys we were meeting? Kathi Jo obviously liked Blake: what if Blake and his friends didn't like me? Would Kathi Jo ditch me this summer?*

We had grown so close over the summer last year, but nine months apart was a long time. She had changed in many ways: she looked older, and more mature than when I saw her last.

Even though she and her mom had just moved to this side of Hillendale last year, she seemed to know the whole place better than I did. I'd never ventured this far on foot before, not without my parents.

"Where are we going?" I asked again, glancing behind me in the dark. Soft music played from one of the houses, and the murmurs of tired campers kept me from feeling alone. But still, being out here this late made me a little nervous.

There had been a terrible incident earlier this year, a mass shooting at a local high school. It had happened in Colorado, far from here ... but still. I'd grown somewhat mistrustful of my peers. And young girls walking alone at night felt recklessly dangerous.

"The shelter house. You know the one I mean, right? Near the docks. We're almost there," Kathi Jo said.

I had seen it, a rickety wooden outbuilding fitted with a few broken-down picnic tables. I'd never seen anyone using it before, but then again, my family and I didn't live here year-round.

There was a long, low whistle up ahead, then a boy emerged from between two trees, blocking our path. He was tall and muscular, wearing only a pair of corduroy shorts. No shirt.

"You made it," he said.

He was smiling as he walked toward us. Even in the dark, I could see that his teeth were very white. Right out of a toothpaste commercial.

Two shadows followed behind him.

"Of course we did," Kathi Jo said. I watched my best friend take off at full speed, running toward the tall, dark stranger. She leapt into his arms and wrapped her legs around his narrow waist. He gripped her firmly in his arms and squeezed her butt.

This must be Blake, then.

Finally, he let Kathi Jo back down onto her feet. She looked over her shoulder at me, her smile giddy and wolfish, gleaming. This was a side of Kathi Jo I'd never seen, a role she hadn't played. The giddy schoolgirl, lost in love and on top of the world.

"Guys, this is my best friend in the whole wide world, Willow. The one I'm always talking about," Kathi Jo said.

Something warm rushed through me then, a sense of belonging and pride. *Her best friend in the whole wide world. And even though she's been here all year without me, meeting new friends and going to her new school, doing new and exciting things … she hasn't forgotten about me. She had even told them about me already!*

"Hi." I waved nervously at the group, shifting from foot to foot. I suddenly wished I'd worn shorts instead, or one of Kathi Jo's thin, cotton dresses. I was sweating, my jeans chafing my inner thighs.

"I'm Blake. Glad we finally get to meet." Blake stepped closer, fully illuminated in the glow of the nearest streetlamp. He smiled at me and stuck out his hand. I shook it and smiled back.

His gaze lingered a little long for comfort, his eyes studying my own. His hands were soft, as though they were covered in baby powder.

"Glad to meet you, too," I said, shifting my view to the other boys.

They looked younger than Blake; one heavyset boy with red hair and freckles, the other skinny with blond hair and a baby face.

"This is Tommy and Trevor," Blake said. "They're assholes."

"Fuck you," the skinny one named Tommy said, reaching for Blake in the dark. Blake ducked and laughed, sweeping behind the smaller boy, and putting him in some sort of chokehold.

"Ignore them. They're on the wrestling team," Kathi Jo said. With her southern accent, it sounded like "rasslin" instead of "wrestling".

I could see the shelter twenty feet ahead, gloomy and ruinous in the dark.

But the boys kept going, Kathi Jo and I skipping to keep up, as they snuck around it.

"Thought we'd go to the tower instead. We'll have more privacy there." Blake winked at me over his shoulder. I felt a strange flutter in my chest.

The world is full of boys like Blake. Privileged and pretty. Charming. I could tell he wasn't low income like many of the other residents in Hillendale. His expensive watch gave him away, as well as the name brand shoes on his feet, the doughy hands, and the designer haircut.

But there was something about him, something different … I couldn't put my finger on what it was. I could see exactly why Kathi Jo was drawn to him because I was drawn to him too.

"I hope there's libations where we're going," Kathi Jo shout-whispered, too loud in my ear. She seemed different around the boys, a more manic version of herself. Perhaps she was simply trying too hard to look cool.

Trevor, the heavier boy with the freckles, led the way, taking a sharp right behind the shelter, entering a gap between two trees in the forest surrounding the lake. From here, the water looked haunting and surreal, reflecting the moonlight on its surface, giving me vertigo. The smell of water and brine filled my nostrils. *These are the scents of summer,* I thought, headily.

There were boats tied up at all the docks, knocking

against wooden beams, the water sloshing noisily like a storm was coming.

I'd never been to any tower in Hillendale, but my interest was piqued. What sort of tower is it? I wondered. With my writer brain, my thoughts instantly fluttered to images of Rapunzel. *High in the sky and all alone, waiting for someone to save her...*

The path through the forest was narrow, but well beaten down. I wondered how often they came here.

"Is it safe?" I whispered to Kathi Jo. She was in front of me now, towering so high above me with her long legs that I couldn't see the boys up ahead. If she'd heard me, she didn't let on.

We walked for what felt like miles, me clumsily trying to avoid branches, sticker bushes, and roots on the foot path; trying not to skin the back of Kathi Jo's heels as I walked behind her.

Finally, the path widened, and I saw a shiny playground in the middle of the forest, along with a cluster of paint-peeled picnic tables.

"I had no idea this was even here," I said, stopping alongside the others and bending down to tie my shoelaces.

There was a tall metal slide; one of the ruthless kinds that tears up your backside and burns the back of your thighs whenever it's above eighty degrees. There were a few swings and a teeter totter, and a big metal merry-go-round that had definitely seen better days. It creaked eerily, and despite the heat, I felt a shiver run down my spine. I wondered why I'd never been here before … *maybe Mom and Dad weren't aware of it on our yearly trips*, I reflected

"Ready?" Blake asked. He looked at Kathi Jo and the boys when he said it, but his eyes drifted over to mine. There was something strange in the way he looked at me, an intensity that made me uncomfortable, but not in a way that felt wholly unpleasant. *Almost like he was studying me, waiting for me to say or do something specific … but what exactly?* I wondered.

"Yep. I'm ready!" Kathi Jo said. She slipped off her shoes and tossed them over by the slide. "Let us go first. That way if we girls fall backwards, or step on a rickety stair, you guys can catch us," she said, flashing that new, wolfish grin of hers.

"Where are we going?" I said, looking around.

But then I saw it—we weren't going to act like kids, taking turns on the slide and spinning each other till we threw up on the merry-go-round. No … we were headed for the fire tower.

I could see it in the distance, a steely monster reaching for the sky. It had to be nearly 50 feet tall.

"It's fifty-six feet," Blake said, reading my mind. "One

thousand and thirty-five feet above sea level though, if you think of it that way. It was built in like the 1930s or something. Isn't it badass?" His face was too close to mine, his breath tickling my cheek. He smelled like summer—honeysuckle and heartache.

"Yeah ... it's ... wow," I said. I looked over at Kathi Jo, but she was busy, digging around in her bag for her one-hitter pipe.

"Y'all ready?" Tommy asked. He had a lit cigarette in his mouth. In the moonlit clearing I could see him more clearly now—he was handsome. Not Blake-handsome, but good-looking all the same, in a rough-around-the-edges sort of way. I considered him for a moment ... *wouldn't it be cool if I had a boyfriend here, too?*

My hands were shaking, and my legs felt numb as we approached the megalith tower. It looked ancient and otherworldly, out of place in this thick, black forest. Looking up from the bottom, I counted dozens of metal stairways. I had vertigo already.

"There are more than a hundred steps. Isn't it awesome?" Tommy whispered; his lips close to my ear.

I was too scared to respond.

"Let's go!" Kathi Jo beamed. She was first up the steps, and I scooted in behind her. As we climbed the first set of stairs, I could smell Tommy right behind me. That honeysuckle heartache smell, or something...

I hesitated as we approached the second set of steps. Tommy placed a hand on the small of my back. "I'm right behind you. I won't let anything bad happen, I promise," he said.

Oh, Tommy … if that were only true.

Chapter Six

SUMMERTIME SADNESS

CURRENT DAY

Time froze.

The honking calls of tree frogs in the woods faded away. The chilly hum of the air conditioner through the vents dissipated. I couldn't see or hear or feel anything ... because Tommy was standing in front of me.

Tommy. Even after all these years, seeing his face triggered something in my mind ... something friendly and familiar, but also fearful. A warning deep in my chest. He smelled the same. What was it I used to write in my journals about the boys of summer? *Honeysuckle and heartache.* Poetic, yet how silly of me...

"What the hell are you doing here, Tommy?" I said, voice shaking.

"Nice to see you too, Willow." When he smiled, I could see the change—a spiderweb of wrinkles around his mouth, a thickening in his jowls. And as he stepped closer to me, taking up the entire doorway, I saw his dark brown hair was turning grey at the temples and growing thin on top. The skinny, young boy was gone—replaced with a solid, real-life man. A grown-up. *Kathi Jo never grew old*, I thought, my heart clenching in my chest.

"I'm sorry... It's just... It's been so long," I said, breathlessly.

"Yeah, it has." Tommy was standing at the top of the rickety stairwell, one hand gripping the rail, the other hanging onto the doorframe. It was a thin front stoop for anyone, but especially a man of his size and stature.

He glanced behind him and down at the parking lot below, as though he were afraid of heights. *Not so brave anymore, huh?* I thought.

I had a strange thought—him falling backward, eyes widening as I watched him go ... *no, no, no*. I shook that thought away.

I peeked over the rail at the parking lot behind him. My Jetta was still the only one out there. How did he get here?

"I walked. I don't live that far from here," Tommy said, reading my mind.

I stepped back and waved him on in, still unable to process that he was here. *Tommy is here, standing in my living room, and Kathi Jo is dead. She's dead and someone left her there, stowed away like trash in my closet … her body pristine … was it some sort of message? A message to me?*

Tommy was too big for my tiny apartment. He stumbled around, looking for a place to sit. Finally, he settled for a wooden chair at my two-person dinette table, his knees scraping the underside of the little table. I snatched up the paper of pointless, rambling questions and tucked it inside my kitchen drawer.

I couldn't sit; my body was bubbling, a mixture of pleasure and pain flowing through my bloodstream. It was nice to see Tommy again, after all these years, but not under these circumstances.

"I heard about the body," Tommy said. He rubbed his thick fingers through his sparse hair, finally resting his chin on his fist.

"How?" I said, pulling out the chair opposite him and sitting down with a deep sigh.

Tommy leaned forward and took something from his back pocket. A wallet. When he opened it, I saw his badge.

I frowned. Strange, that the boy who smoked pot and climbed towers at midnight with me and my friends was now in charge of picking up kids our age for doing the same thing. But then again … there was something about him being a cop that felt right. He always was the nicest of the boys; the only one who seemed responsible or had any sense.

"I didn't see you at the house earlier though…" I said, eyes roaming the shiny badge.

"It's my night off. Or it was supposed to be. Buddy of mine called me the moment you called it in, so I had to come see you first. Had to make sure you're okay before I went down there myself," Tommy said.

I closed my eyes, not wanting to see Kathi Jo's face again but having no other choice. *Those eyes, that waxen face … but how? How did she look the same after all these years? Did someone preserve her body? WHO?!*

"Are you sure it was her?" Tommy asked. His fingers brushed against my forearm, and I pulled away, leaning back in my chair. He, like the rest of us, had been upset when Kathi Jo left. He helped search for her back then… Everyone did. Except me, because I'd been whisked back home to Branton at the end of summer.

"It's definitely her," I said, pinching my eyes closed. "I wish it wasn't."

Tommy sat back too, rubbing his face in his hands. "But … how? And why now, and why your place?"

I shook my head. "I don't know. I've been asking myself the same questions. All this time, we thought she'd run away. But we were wrong … so wrong."

"Is it possible that her body's been inside your parents' lake house all these years?" Tommy asked.

My eyes narrowed. "You know she hasn't been in the lake house! That's impossible. The house hasn't sat empty all this time, my parents rented it out off and on for several years, and there were maintenance people and lawncare folks who showed up regularly... Plus, my construction workers would have found it... Someone must have placed it there. And the body..."

"What about the body?" he asked.

I tried to read the expression on his face. His eyes were full of alarm, his interest so intense that it frightened me. *Could he have had something to do with Kathi Jo's death back then? After all this time ... what if her killer was living right here in Hillendale?*

"The body didn't smell," I told him. Closing my eyes again, I tried to conjure up the scene—mine and Cindy's horrific discovery. I tried to remember what it smelled like. "There was no smell at all. Well, a little dank and dusty, like the smell of an old closet..."

I'd always considered myself a "good smeller"; a teacher of mine in a high school biology class had conducted a "super smeller" test during a lesson, and I'd done better than anyone else. If Kathi Jo's body had smelled like rot, even the least little bit, I would have sniffed it out. The odor would be burned in my nostril hairs right about now...

"She's been missing, for what? Fifteen years?" Tommy asked.

"It would have been twenty-two years this summer," I said, softly.

"Twenty-two years... Wouldn't the body be...?" Tommy cringed.

"Her flesh would be gone, rotted to the bone. Bone turning into dust... Someone must have preserved her. Otherwise, this makes no sense." I scratched my head. The cops and paramedics had ushered both Cindy and me out of there; now I wished I'd taken a closer look at the actual body before we called the cops.

"It looked just like she did back then ... dark hair and piercings, pale skin. Black clothes ... like she died only yesterday."

"I can't believe someone killed her," Tommy said, jaw flinching.

I was about to respond when I heard the thud of a car door downstairs. Tommy and I sat still, listening as someone climbed the metallic stairs to my apartment door.

I had the strangest thought—what if it's her killer? Coming to take us too? Revenge for what happened that summer?

There was a loud knock on the front door. Since returning to Hillendale, I hadn't had one visitor at my apartment. Now, in the span of an hour, I'd had two.

Three, I realized, when I opened the door. Two more police officers, these ones in uniform, clustered together on the metal stoop.

"Mrs. Roberts?"

"That's me," I said, opening the door for them. One of the officers was an older, white-haired gentleman. I thought he looked vaguely familiar. The other was a young female who looked barely old enough to be out of high school. Both officers looked past me toward the dinette at Tommy.

The older officer nodded silently at Tommy, then turned back to me.

"I'm Officer Spanos and this is Officer Beckham," the older one said. "Can we come in for a few minutes? We'd like to discuss the thing we found at the house over on Daisy Lane."

I opened the door and motioned for them to come inside. They, too, looked too large for this space.

"What do you mean, 'thing'? That seems like an unnecessarily cruel way to refer to the body of my former best friend," I said, crossing my arms over my chest.

The young policewoman was looking over at Tommy, giving him a strange, frightened look. She cleared her throat and turned towards me. "Ma'am, what we found at the lake house wasn't a body."

SUMMER OF '99

That's how we spent our summer—nights were reserved for the fire tower. We drank triple sec and apple pucker, because that's all we could get sometimes. Both burned on the way down; I imagined a gaping hole in my esophagus ripping and tearing beneath the skin. I hated the feeling of getting drunk, giving up control of my body and mind when I barely had full control over those things when I was sober.

Blake taught me how to play gin rummy and I taught them all how to dance. I even lugged my 15lb boom box up the countless stairs of the tower, and played Outkast, Dr. Dre, and Eminem.

Tommy told stories about the tower, how local legend claimed that if you looked out far enough, from the top of the tower, you could sometimes see the fires burning. Fires lit by devil worshippers who snuck into Hillendale and sacrificed young girls for their rituals.

I always hated those stories and never once did I see any fires. But still, the fear was always there until I blurred it away with pot and alcohol.

Most nights were just that—a blur—and by the time we came stumbling home, Kathi Jo and I slipping through her back door and crawling up the stairs to her second-floor bedroom, we could barely contain our giggles.

It was hot that summer, the box fan always stirring. Our sticky thighs stuck together like fly ribbon underneath the sheets.

Although the nights were for the boys, the daytime was ours. Just the two of us again, like old times. Most mornings, by the time Kathi Jo and I rolled out of bed, hung over but young and healthy enough to cope, her mom was gone to work. If she knew we were sneaking out at night, she never said so.

Would she have stopped us if she had?

In hindsight, I realized, *she probably would have.*

My mother, too, was silent when it came to my late nights with Kathi Jo. We rarely stayed at my place anymore, and my parents didn't seem to mind that. Some nights, when we came lurching through the trees, I could hear them over there fighting inside the stone house. I wasn't sure what they argued about, but it was almost a *relief* to hear something coming out of them. Anything but that dead, awkward silence I'd grown to dread. Some late mornings and afternoons when Kathi Jo and I went back to my place for lunch, Dad wasn't there. *At the casino*, my mother told me one time. *He must have been doing well if he stayed all night.*

I knew they weren't getting along. Deep down, it worried me, but also … I had these late-night fantasies— that if they got divorced, Dad would stay here in Hillendale full-time, and I could live here with him.

Mom made the best turkey sandwiches, topped with lots of mayo and cheese and sweet rye bread. Kathi Jo and I often walked over to my house for lunch. We left Mom on her own to eat, taking our sandwiches, and sometimes cookies, down to the lakeshore.

We swam a lot that summer, nearly every day, my sunburn turning crispy then golden brown. And like the year before that, we made up stories, going out on the kayak, venturing further than ever before.

We collected shells all along the shoreline and dug for crawdads in the creeks.

"He's perfect, right?" Kathi Jo asked me once, tossing a baby crawdad in an old coffee can. They were cute little things, but they had pinchers. If you grabbed them by the front or the tail end, it hurt.

"The crawdad is perfect?" I laughed. But I knew who she meant. *And yes. Yes, Blake's perfect.*

"Blake, silly!" Kathi Jo said.

"I knew who you meant. Yeah, he's pretty cool, I guess. Is he your boyfriend now?" I couldn't get a read on the two of them. Sure, it was obvious how Kathi Jo felt about him, but how did he feel about her?

Sometimes, I got the sense that he thought of her like a little sister.

But, then again, there were those nights when we stayed out until nearly daylight, and I could see them kissing, drunkenly swaying on the playground, or squished together in the top of the tower.

"I think he is," Kathi Jo said. She lifted another crawdad, a chubby old thing, and pretended to chase me with it.

"Don't you dare!" I squealed.

But Kathi Jo always dared, and the next thing I knew we were running through the trees. Our laughter was our never-ending summer soundtrack. My favorite song loop of all time.

Chapter Seven

PLAYING DRESS-UP

CURRENT DAY

"I don't understand." I tried to back up, to get away from these liars, but I stepped right into Tommy. He rested his hands, strong and steady on my shoulders, holding me still. I'd never wanted so badly for him *not* to touch me.

What we found at the lake house wasn't a body...

No, that couldn't be true.

"I saw her. It was real. Are you sure you checked in the right place?" It was a stupid question—obviously, they had checked. But my words were moving faster than my brain could process the thoughts. *Here I am still trying to process the discovery of my childhood best friend's body, and now they want me to process this claim that all of it was fake?*

"What do you mean, it wasn't a body?" Tommy asked the other officers. His voice seemed calm. Too calm.

I allowed myself to sink into him; he wrapped his arms all the way around me and for a moment, the feeling of faintness faded.

"It was a mannequin," the older officer—Officer Spanos—said, grimly.

A mannequin?!

I shook my head back and forth, back and forth. "No fucking way it was a mannequin. I saw it! It looked just like her ... no! Didn't you see the septum piercing? Her black hair... No, I don't believe you..."

The female cop—Officer Beckham, I believed—stepped forward and held out her phone like a peace offering. "It's okay, Willow. Here. Let me show you."

She thumbed in her passcode, swiped a couple times, and lifted the phone in front of my face.

"Please, I can't look again..." I begged.

"It's not real, I promise. But it looks real as fuck, right?" I was startled by her words, her demeanor. She could have been one of my co-workers at Camelot primary school where I'd taught: prim and proper in the classroom and then chatting it up like sailors in the teacher's lounge. Holding up their phones to show me something stupid on YouTube.

"Come on. Let's sit down and I'll show you and explain," Officer Beckham said. I let her lead me by the elbow over to the dingy loveseat that smelled like cat piss and carp.

I forced myself to look at what she wanted to show me, wriggling uncomfortably in my seat.

"See right here?" She zoomed in on Kathi Jo's face—no, not Kathi Jo. The *dummy*'s face. "It's made of some sort of silicone. Or plastic, maybe. This isn't some cheap Halloween toy you buy off Amazon. This is the real deal."

"The real deal?" I swallowed, eyes scanning the waxy looking image. She was right—seeing it in a photo, under bright lights instead of through a plastic sheath in the dark, gave it a stiff, unrealistic look. *That would explain the lack of smell…*

But the piercing, the tattoo, the hair…

My eyes fluttered up and down the picture. Officer Beckham zoomed in and out, accommodating my curiosity.

There were no tattoos on the "body", no sex characteristics. It looked real but wasn't. The only thing that actually resembled Kathi Jo was the dummy's hair, the metal piercing, black clothing, and teenage size.

I'd assumed there would be a tattoo after seeing the septum piercing. That eerie black octopus, moving back and forth on Kathi Jo's thigh bone…

The more I looked at the photo, the more I understood. There were no holes in the mannequin's ears … only a shiny brass ring on the septum that looked similar, but not the same, as the one I remembered Kathi Jo wearing when we were teens. It was like, I saw the body and my brain filled in the gaps, jumping to the wrong conclusion…

"But … I still don't understand. Why would someone do this to me?"

Officer Spanos cleared his throat. He and Tommy were standing in the living room, watching my reaction to the photos. "We were hoping you could explain that to us. Hoping you could tell us how that dummy got in there."

"Me? I wouldn't know the first thing about buying a mannequin, and I sure as hell wouldn't place one that looked like my missing best friend at my own property that I'm fixing to sell." As I looked around my tiny, cramped apartment filled with people, all of a sudden, nothing seemed real anymore. The room was dingier, the curves of the ceiling and the dust on the shelves … it was like I was seeing it all for the first time.

Why in the hell did I come back to Hillendale? I could have let them do the work without me here… I could have found somewhere else to go, somewhere far from my soon-to-be-ex. I'm back and now it's all going to shit again… This place, it brings out those old memories. And it brings out the worst in people...

Old memories and old pain; there's something about old pain that is sneaky. It shows up when you least expect it, hitting a different nerve each time...

I'd loved her once. My best friend. And as relieved as I was to know she wasn't dead, wrapped in plastic, the alternative made no sense either. *Why would someone do this to me? Were they trying to send a message or was this some sort of sick prank?*

"Over the years, have you heard anything from Kathi Jo Redfield? She was reported as a runaway twenty-two years ago" Officer Beckham's words hit like sharp shock waves.

"No, of course not. No one has, as far as I know... She left town after what happened. She couldn't deal, supposedly... There was even a note..."

"But?" Officer Beckham leaned forward. She looked too young to know this case, to remember what it was like—what it *felt* like—for all of us when Kathi Jo disappeared. It didn't feel like a runaway situation.

At first, I thought: *Kathi Jo wouldn't leave me behind even though she was upset about what I did that night... She just wouldn't. She wouldn't!*

But it didn't take long for me to realize how wrong I was. Kathi Jo didn't take much with her, but she left a note for her mom. And it wasn't the first time she'd threatened to run away.

"I thought she ran away, just like everyone else did. But then I saw that body tonight and I thought finally, we would get some answers," I said, the words like whispers in the stuffy apartment.

Officer Spanos sighed. "Unfortunately, there are only more questions at this point. Such as, who would put a dummy that resembled a missing girl in your closet? And most importantly, why?"

My eyes moved from him to Tommy. Tommy had a stake in this too. But he was silent, arms crossed over his chest, eyes faraway and misty. Was it fear I saw there? Or was it sadness? Once upon a time, he'd loved her too. We all had.

"I have no idea who or why. But if you find out the answers, I'd like to know," I said. Tommy looked at me, his eyes sharp now.

The windowpanes were rattling, a storm outside gaining momentum. Tommy said, "I don't understand why anyone would do this. There's nothing about a fake dead body."

I watched him, seeing not the cop or the middle-aged man, but the smiley boy from my youth. Memories of that last night fluttering back to me...

Fingers dancing in the dark. Secrets between the sheets. And a body that needed to be hidden.

What did I know about this new Tommy? Tommy the tough guy. Tommy the cop. I didn't think he was capable of pulling off a sick prank like this, nor did I see any motive for him to do it. *But how well do I know him now... Did I really ever know him back then?*

Truth is, he didn't know me either. Or of what I was capable.

SUMMER OF '99

"Tell me about your tattoos," I said.

Kathi Jo had told me a bit once, that first summer, but I wanted to hear it again. All the details. It's not every day you see a girl our age with piercings and a tattoo. They had occurred on her father's watch, and apparently, her mom had been pissed. They were both wild, Kathi Jo had told me one night, showing me a picture of her mom and dad. Her dad was handsome, in a rugged way, and her mother had looked stunning on the motorcycle behind him in the photo, hair wind-blown and dressed in tight leather.

"When I was born, my mother changed. The whole biker life, the tattoos, and the wild nights ... she was done with all that. A baby changes things. At least it changed things for her...

"But my dad refused to change. For a while, I spent every weekend with him at his apartment. But Mom put a stop to that, especially after the tattoo and piercings. And Dad gave up on me, I guess. Moved out of town, started up his own little family elsewhere. I tried to run away a few times to get his attention. Once, I even hopped on a bus and made it halfway to his house before the cops caught me and hauled me back to Mom," Kathi Jo said.

I tried to imagine her father somewhere else, another family filled with leather and motors, late-night bike rides in the rain.

I felt terrible for bringing up the tattoo, and with it memories of her absent father.

"I'm so sorry. That must be so hard…"

Kathi Jo shrugged and continued with her story. "My dad's roommate was a tattoo and piercing artist. I think I told you that, didn't I?" Kathi Jo asked. We were sprawled out on my bed in the loft, stripped down to only panties and t-shirts as we waited for our bathing suits to dry in the dryer downstairs.

It was so hot that summer, the box fan always running on high. And we were always sweating, no matter how we tried to cool down from the heat. We swam so much in the daytime; it's not like we had a choice—it was the only way to escape the blistering midday sun. So, our bathing suits were constantly needing to be dried, spinning carelessly in the dryer or strung up out back on the clothesline.

"Yeah, you told me that. But that's all you said. I want to know everything. Like, did it hurt? And why did you choose the art that you did? How does one come up with shit like that?" I was trying out more and more cuss words that summer, but they always felt weird in my mouth. Like someone else was saying them for me.

We were lying head to foot, alongside each other. I reached out, my fingertips skimming the top of her thigh, the thick black tentacles of her octopus tattoo. As cool as the piercings and the tattoo were, I couldn't help wondering if Kathi Jo was playing dress-up. Trying to be someone she wasn't, trying to prove something to herself, or to her parents. *Look, Dad. Mom has changed but I haven't. I'm still cool! Please don't leave me for a new family.*

It broke my heart to think about it, but I would never dare say that to her.

Kathi Jo shivered at my touch but didn't move away. "His roommate was younger than him. Sexy as fuck, too. So, I let him do the tattoo one night, and then the piercings another night. Dad was drunk during most of it, but he thought they looked pretty cool when he woke up and saw them. It hurt, the tattoo … but not as much as the aftermath. My mom was so pissed. Not at me, but at Dad for letting it happen."

"Why did you choose an octopus though?" I asked, hoping to steer the conversation in a brighter direction.

"Well, octopi are smart creatures. They're solitary and

they don't rely on anyone for anything. They're super resourceful, too; they can outwit most predators. I think they're the most intelligent invertebrate in the ocean. Plus, they look pretty badass too, don't you think?" She flexed her thigh, moving it side to side, creating the illusion that the octopus was moving. I could almost believe that it was alive, a monstrous creature hiding underwater. Perhaps the kind of monster that doesn't want to be found, happy in its own hidden den.

"They don't live long though, do they?" I touched it again, trying to remember what I'd learned about octopi in my oceanography elective last year. Not much. I'd spent most of the class doodling notes and stories on paper, instead of listening to old Mr. Crum's monotonous teaching voice. It felt so long ago, as though more than a year had passed. Everything seemed to change so quickly at this age. At least one thing had stayed the same—our friendship.

"I don't know. Maybe some of them live forever... I mean, what do we really know about the deep dark sea anyway? Everything about them is a mystery, an enigma ... just like me," Kathi Jo said, wiggling her toes at me.

Before I could respond, she was on her feet, jumping up and down on my bed, smacking her hands on the low ceiling above. "I'm bored. Let's go see the boys."

There it was. Her preoccupation with Blake and the others. I resented it when we were together, just the two of us, but I always had fun when I was with them too. Summer was reaching its end, anyway, and I only had another week before I had to return to the trailer park in Branton. It didn't seem fair, the thought of having to leave. Why do they get to stay behind while the rest of us out-of-towners return to everyday life?

I liked my school okay back home in Branton, but I didn't have many friends there—at least not the kind you could stay up all night talking to, sharing your secrets with.

Kathi Jo bounced on the bed, using her knees, and I couldn't help smiling.

"Okay, let's go," I said in surrender. "But promise me we won't stay out all night. I still want to crawl in bed one night before I leave town and watch *Titanic* with you. All three and a half hours of it."

Kathi Jo used to joke that it was "actually four hours, counting those damn previews", but today, she seemed preoccupied.

Already off the bed, she was tugging on her jean shorts and Nike slide sandals.

"We'll watch it later. I promise," she said, digging through her purse for a tube of lipstick.

Chapter Eight

FALLING

CURRENT DAY

That night, with Tommy and the police gone, finally, I sat down on my bed and opened my laptop. My inbox was full—mostly junk mail, but there were a couple private messages from co-workers at the school wishing me well. *Good luck with your next steps. Wishing you the best on your journey.*

But what steps might those be? And where was this "journey" going to lead me?

I'd left my job on a whim; but it wasn't like I'd had a choice. When your husband is the principal and you're a lowly part-time teacher with only a few years under your belt, it's obvious whose reputation and job security take precedence.

It was unsettling how quickly it happened—my entire "friends" group disintegrating before my very eyes when Jason and I announced our split. It didn't take long for me to realize that most of our friends were his friends, and virtually all were associated with the school. I hated leaving the place, but Jason hadn't left me much choice; he had threatened on multiple occasions to destroy my reputation if I stayed. Before I left town, I was worried less about the job and more for my physical safety.

It was an overwhelming feeling … being jobless again for the first time in many years. But the nice thing about having my teaching certificate was that I could use it elsewhere. I didn't have to stick around that school anymore, working in the same town—or even the same state—as Jason, with his phony smile in public and his eyes, hard like metal, behind closed doors.

But, clearly, returning to Hillendale had been a mistake. I hadn't even checked out the local school system or checked for open positions in the county. I'd been so focused on getting the lake house up and running so I could rent it out and establish some income before summer arrived. The thought of never having to rely on Jason, or any other man, for extra income again appealed to me greatly.

But now it'd all been shot to shit with this mannequin stunt.

Certainly, word about it had already spread through

the close-knit town of Hillendale. People would start to wonder about Kathi Jo again.

Although some of us never really stopped.

~

The morning air felt heavy and warm on my skin as I crossed the walking bridge, retracing my steps from last night.

The water of Lake Hillendale was calm below my feet, smooth as glass and devoid of fishermen or boaters this time of year. The smell of rain clung to the air, wet and warm in my lungs. Another storm was coming, perhaps in more ways than one.

The bridge creaked under me, a warning. Mom used to warn us not to take Holman's Bridge to the other side of the lake, but it had always held and here I was, decades later, still gripping the same ropy handrails and edging across it despite my better judgement.

So many of us had fallen apart, but the bridge still stood. Sometimes, people and places will surprise you—what stays and what goes…

As I walked, my boots cast shadows on the sunlit surface. The bridge seemed safer during the day, somehow. The whole town did.

I felt a rush of relief—just as I had in my youth—when I made it safely to the other side. It took fewer than fifteen minutes to reach the lake house from my apartment. In the light of day, my path felt different—I wasn't rushing in response to a call about a body this time, thank God. But I was dreading my return to the house, unsure of what I expected to find now that the cops were gone.

The house looked quiet as I approached through the woods, sullen and alone, this stocky stone house hidden in the trees. With no crew members on site or work trucks clumped up in the driveway, it looked different. It looked the way it used to—Mom and Dad behind those doors, silent and brooding. A war of silence, or a war of words … their anger stretching at the seams…

I let myself in with my key and walked through the kitchen and living room, flipping on lights despite the natural daylight seeping in.

It was the only place I could truly call "home"; the only house I'd ever owned. I thought back to my house with Jason, with its white-washed walls and cheap, cookie-cutter cabinets on its half-lot surrounded by identical houses. It had never felt like home. Jason had picked the place, one of those hoity-toity neighborhoods where everybody knows your name and wants to fine you if your grass is a centimeter too long. We had never owned that house; rather, it owned us, and we paid for the privilege of saying we lived there.

But my fishy apartment on the other side of the lake was a far cry from homey either…

Slowly, I approached the main bedroom of the lake house, heart thudding in my chest. I could still see Kathi Jo's body there in my mind, so clearly, face stretched behind a thin sheath of plastic, a hideous mask of horror … but no, it wasn't real. It wasn't Kathi Jo in that closet.

There were muddy boot prints on the floor where the officers had trampled through last night. The door to the closet was closed. I approached it, took a breath, and flung the doors wide open.

No body inside this time. Thank God.

The police had removed the imposter version of Kathi Jo. All that remained were the same hangers and dust bunnies from before. Even the plastic bag the dummy had been contained in was gone.

For a moment, I could almost believe that it had all been an awful dream. A figment of my imagination.

I shut the closet tight and shut off the lights, closing the bedroom door behind me.

The windy metal stairs to the loft were dusty from disuse. I gripped the cold metal handrail and climbed. I used to charge up and down these steps, over and over. But now my out-of-shape knees and legs ached as I reached the top.

As much as I used to dislike the décor in the lake house, I found myself missing it now. At the top of the stairs, I looked back, eyes absorbing the top half of the living room and dining area below. This place used to feel like home at one time; I used to have the perfect view from up here.

I wanted to go back—the dead animals and the floral wallpaper. All of it. I'd even take the cock-a-doodle-doo farm decorations in the kitchen. But all of that was gone now, replaced with a shell of the place it had once been.

Someone had been in here recently; someone had placed that phony doll in the closet. It had to be a message of some kind. I could almost believe it was a teenage prank, but the teens in Hillendale probably didn't even remember a runaway teen from nearly two decades ago. No, it had to be someone who knew her ... someone with inside information about all of us that summer. I was certain of it.

At the very top stair of the loft, I drew in a breath. The renovators hadn't taken out a single thing up here yet. My old mattress still lay limp on the floor, the chunky dresser and decrepit boxed fan still pushed against the corner.

But there was something different. I tried to flip on the ceiling light, but nothing happened. Bulb must have burned out.

I approached the bed, and the note sitting in the center of it.

A ripped piece of paper, torn from a notebook, sat in the middle of the bed.

The loopy letters looked familiar. I covered my mouth with my hand, reading the words:

I know what you did. It's time to come clean about that summer.

SUMMER '99

That's the thing about falling. Once you've lost your footing and submitted to the pull of gravity, it's impossible to slow the momentum.

And it's a lot harder to get back up than it is to fall.

I could see Kathi Jo falling for Blake Ashcroft and falling *hard*. There were traces of who she used to be, my old friend … but she had evolved. Around Blake, she blinked a little slower. Smiled a little wider. With him, she showed all her teeth.

Three nights before I had to leave Hillendale for the summer, we had a change of venue for our nightly excursion. Blake had invited us to his house instead of the fire tower.

I'd never been there before, but I wasn't surprised to learn it was one of the big lakefront properties on the other side of Lake Hillendale. A massive A-frame, it hovered like a giant over the water, wide decks and newly built boat docks extending out like appendages on either side of it.

There were two boats docked at the sides that belonged to the Ashcrofts; not what people called yachts, but they were certainly what I considered a yacht. Both boats were larger than my family's trailer back home in Branton. And cars. There was a whole line of them parked in the half roundabout—I didn't know what kind. I never knew those sorts of things, only that they were shiny and expensive.

"Blake has three brothers. All older than him," Kathi Jo said, fingers brushing over the red paint of a shiny sports car as we approached the grand entranceway.

"Will they be here tonight?" For a moment, I felt a glimmer of hope. Maybe Blake had an older brother just like him—not rich, I didn't care about that. But he was handsome and funny. Confident. I wouldn't mind finding a cute, funny guy of my own that was similar to Blake, but less douchey.

"Nah. His brothers are partying in Greenville tonight. College students. Too cool for us, I guess," she said.

"What about his parents? Don't they mind that we're here?" I tried to imagine my own parents granting my friends and me permission to get drunk and act stupid in a nice place like this. My parents might have been careless and neglectful when it came to my nightly activities, but they certainly wouldn't have agreed to actively sign off on them. They were too morally superior, in their own minds, for that.

I was wearing a baby doll dress and leather sandals I'd borrowed from Kathi Jo's closet. My hair was braided, in an attempt to look effortlessly pretty. Most important was what lay beneath my clothes—a tiny blue bikini with yellow bows on the hips. I'd begged Mom to take me into town, for once doing an activity that didn't involve Kathi Jo. Each summer at the lake, we had both worn one-piece bathing suits—pretty and colorful, but conservative all the same.

Tonight, I wanted to shock them all with my new bikini. All the walking over summer had made me feel taller, leaner. I wanted to show off my new, blossoming figure in the pool and hot tub at Blake's tonight—*but who am I showing off for, exactly?* I wondered.

My throat was dry, and my stomach rumbled noisily as Kathi Jo rang the bell. I'd barely eaten today, just chips and a yogurt; I'd been so eager to look thin in my bikini, but now I wished I had eaten more. Half a drink and I'd be drunk if I weren't careful.

"You look pretty." Kathi Jo nudged me with her shoulder. I felt a flash of guilt, for not taking her with me to the boat gear shop on Harlan Street. We could have picked out matching bikinis together, maybe.

"Thanks. So do you." Kathi Jo was wearing plaid khaki shorts and a thin, lacy tank top that showed off her budding cleavage. *Her and Blake look good together*, I realized. *Like the homecoming king and queen. And I'm their token trailer park trash friend.*

Before I could process those dark feelings of envy, the massive front double doors of Blake's house swung open. I was surprised to see, not the boys, but a young blonde girl at the door.

"Hello, ladies!" She grinned. She looked older and more mature than us; it only took a split second for me to realize she was Blake's sister. She had the same buttery-blonde hair, athletic build, and dove-grey eyes that Blake had.

I wondered why Kathi Jo hadn't mentioned a sister, and why she had never come to the fire tower or down to the lake to hang out with us.

"Hi! Chloe, this is my friend Willow," Kathi said, adjusting her backpack on her shoulders in the doorway. Chloe scrunched up her nose and tilted her head.

"That's an interesting name," she said, curiously. But the way she said it didn't make me feel interesting at all. "You must not be a regular because I've never seen you at school."

I shot Kathi Jo a sideways glance. How come she hadn't mentioned me to Blake's sister?

And while we were at it—why hadn't Blake or the other guys mentioned me, either?

"I live in Branton, but my family comes up here to visit every summer. Nice to meet you, Chloe," I said.

"You too." The judgy look was gone, her bright toothpaste smile beaming.

"Well, make yourselves at home," she said, widening the door for us to enter. "Mom and my big brothers are gone, and Dad's getting ready to leave for a weekend work trip. We'll have this whole place to ourselves."

As I stepped into the foyer, taking it all in, I tried to hide my astonishment. The house was colossal, high ceilings in the open-air living room reaching at least twenty feet. There were dual staircases at the center of the room, each leading up to a second-floor landing that was topped off with the sparkliest, most ornate chandelier I'd ever seen.

Kathi Jo had been here once before; she'd told me on the way over. She had also warned me that Blake's family was loaded. But there's a difference between rich and *rich* rich. Blake's family definitely fell in the latter category.

We followed Chloe down a long, dimly lit hallway with closed rooms on either side of it. I smelled the pool before I saw it, the chlorine stinging my nostrils and reminding me of easier times, when I was younger, swimming with Mom at the local public pool in my floaties, or when Kathi Jo and I would venture out on the "dangerous seas" of Hillendale in our mighty, unsinkable "ship".

I gasped when I saw the pool. It was more than a pool —rather, it was a huge natatorium, enclosed in thick, steamy glass and surrounded by luxurious loungers. Tommy, Trevor, and Blake were in a hot tub next to the pool, all three of them shirtless clutching dark brew beers in their fists. Rap music played, booming from elaborate speakers in every corner. The sound was everywhere— around me and inside me, and the whole steamy, loud space made me feel a tad disoriented, and a whole lot overwhelmed.

"Finally! Someone more interesting than these clowns," Blake said, lifting up his beer to wave at us. Trevor and Tommy were beside him, drinking too. They both smiled at me and waved.

Chloe came out of nowhere, tucking a wine cooler in my hand. I took a small sip. It was both bitter and sweet; in truth, I hated the taste of alcohol. I wasn't crazy about the way it made me feel either.

The girls were already stripping off their clothes, getting down to their suits to join the boys in the hot tub. I felt hot, my armpits damp with sweat. I looked longingly at the pool, and the slides on the other side of it. I yearned for those younger days, when every girl I knew was more worried about sliding and splashing instead of impressing boys. I took another sip of my drink and slid off my sandals, turning my back on the hot tub. The girls were already getting in; I could hear them splashing, sighing, and giggling with the boys. I wondered if there would even be room in the hot tub for me.

But now was my chance to show off my new swimsuit and slimmer waistline. I lifted the dress over my head and slipped it off, then turned around.

They were staring, all of them, and I felt a rush of excitement and satisfaction. Even a little pride.

"Keep going!" Trevor said, clinking his bottle with Tommy's. Tommy laughed, but then gave me an apologetic smile.

"Keep going, I said!" Trevor repeated. It took me a moment to realize what he meant—that I should take the rest of my clothes off.

"You wish," I said, rolling my eyes. I tightened the string on my bikini top and dipped my toe in the steaming hot water. There was barely any room left, just a tight squeeze between Chloe and Trevor. I slid in, letting the water envelop me, clutching the ice-cold drink.

That's when I realized Chloe wasn't wearing a bathing suit, her breasts floating on the surface of the water. And as I looked around at the others, I realized none of them were either. Even Kathi Jo.

"Hey, I saw that bathing suit on sale at Cristo Mart,"

Kathi Jo said. She pointed at me, eyes slanted through the steam. I noticed her drink was nearly empty already.

When had she gone to Cristo Mart without me? I wondered.

"Oh, really? I don't remember where I got it, actually…"

Chloe giggled. "It's okay. You could admit it if you went out and bought a new bathing suit for tonight! Dress to impress, right?"

My cheeks burned.

"You should have talked to Kat first though. She would have told you we always get in naked. Could have saved you some money," Chloe said.

I took another sip of my drink, trying to hide my embarrassment. The way she said "save you money" made me think she was taking a dig at me for growing up poor. Had Kathi Jo told her about where I lived in Branton? Kathi Jo had never been to visit my trailer back home, but we'd talked about it. She knew how self-conscious it made me, and how much I hated living there.

And the way she talked about their past rendezvous in the hot tub made me think this wasn't only Kathi Jo's second visit.

Perhaps she's been spending more time here than she's letting on. Replacing her old best friend with a new one, I thought.

"Here, let me help you," Trevor said. I felt his fingers on my back, tugging at my string bikini top.

"No! Get off," I said, popping him in the rib with my elbow.

"Prude," Kathi Jo said, laughing.

"Leave her alone, you all," Tommy said, shaking his head back and forth at Trevor.

"You have to forgive my friend. She's a little timid," Kathi Jo said, with a giggle.

This time I didn't try to hide my disappointment. I rolled my eyes and sat the bottle of nasty alcohol on the ground outside the hot tub. Suddenly, all I wanted to do was go back home. Sit up in the loft by myself, working on my stories, listening to tree frogs and crickets outside with the balcony doors wide open. With or without Kathi Jo.

Screw these people and this place, I thought, sullenly.

The next hour passed by in a blur, the others chit-chatting and laughing. Telling jokes I didn't know the punchline to that had to do with their school or their local sports teams. I couldn't shake the feeling that all I wanted to do was close my eyes and fall back, sinking under the steaming hot water, and lie on the bottom of the hot tub floor.

Blake was saddled up next to Kathi Jo and she was eating up every word he said. Blake, Chloe, and Kathi Jo seemed to have forgotten I existed; Tommy, like me, was mostly quiet and watchful. Trevor, on the other hand, kept scooting closer and closer, making me feel uncomfortable. He was always silly and wild, but tonight, he seemed drunker than the others and grossly handsy.

"Can I use your bathroom?" I spoke quietly to Chloe.

She launched into a conversation with Kathi Jo, calling her "Kat" every chance she got, and pretended she didn't hear me. *What a bitch.*

I stood, shaking off the water and stepping out. Trevor let out a low whistle and I gathered up a fluffy white towel from a stack on a brown wicker ottoman and wrapped it around me.

"I'm going to go find a bathroom," I said, not caring if anyone heard.

I slid the screen door open and stepped into the house; the frigid air conditioning gave me instant goosebumps. I wrapped the towel tighter and walked down the long, wide hallway. Water dripped off my legs and hair, making a slick trail behind me, but I didn't care.

I just wanted to close myself in the bathroom and have a good cry.

Everyone and everything around me were changing … and there was nothing I could do about it. I'd never felt so unsure about my friendship with Kathi Jo.

I'd always liked every version of my best friend, but this version—the cool girl who pretended to be on the same level as some snotty rich kids—was my least favorite version of all.

But aren't you trying to do the same thing? Fit in where you don't belong? I chastised myself.

The doors along the hallway were closed, so I started opening them, one by one, as I looked for a bathroom. Now, I actually needed to go, my bladder expanding painfully.

The first door I opened revealed a laundry room that was larger than most of my trailer back home. I closed the door back and moved on. The next two rooms were bedrooms, neat and pristine but plain, as though they'd never been used. I tried to imagine "Kat" hanging out here, taking one of these rooms when she stayed. Better yet, Blake's parents will probably let her curl up into his bed beside him.

When I opened the fourth door, I let out a strangled gasp. An older man sat behind a heavy, mahogany desk; a phone held close to his ear.

"Oh, God! I'm so sorry!" I pulled the door back shut and stumbled down the hallway, looking for somewhere to hide from the man behind the desk who was clearly Blake's father.

Much to my dismay, I heard a door open behind me. When I wheeled around, Blake's dad was there, smiling in the hallway.

"Hey, there! I don't think we've met! I'm Ian." The

man walked toward me and stuck out his hand. He had grey hair and tan skin, those same grey eyes as Chloe and Blake. In his khaki pants and button-down shirt, he looked like a proper businessman. I could see where Blake and Chloe got their good looks from.

"Hi. I'm sorry I walked in on you. I'm Willow. I was looking for the bathroom. This place is so big, somebody could get lost in it…" I accepted his hand in mine. He shook it; not the way you shake a young girl's hand, but with a proper, sturdy, respectful grip.

Ian chuckled. "You're right. It's way too big. And the layout of this place is awful."

"No, I didn't mean that. It's a lovely home…"

Ian waved his hand. "Come on. I'll show you where the bathroom is. I'm guessing you're one of Chloe's friends?"

"I came here with Kathi Jo. I'm friends with Blake, but I had a chance to meet Chloe tonight." I let him lead me down the hallway. A few more doors, and I would have made it.

"Thanks. Nice to meet you." I slipped inside the bathroom, closing the door quickly behind me. My cheeks were hot with embarrassment. I splashed my face and hands in a fancy pedestal sink and stumbled around trying to get my too-tight, wet bottoms off so I could pee.

Blake's dad seemed kind. I wondered why he was

still home—hadn't Chloe mentioned her parents were out? Or did she just say her brothers and mom?

After using the restroom and washing my hands again, I tried to fix my damp braid and I retightened the string on my top. When I opened the bathroom door, I was shocked to find Blake's dad still standing there, waiting for me.

"Oh! You didn't have to wait for me but thank you. I could have found my way back to the pool." My thoughts darkened—perhaps he can tell I'm poor and was worried I might snoop around and try to steal something.

"I'm sure you could have. But I was going to make some hot chocolate in the kitchen for myself and you looked so cold earlier... Would you like a cup?" Ian raised his eyebrows and smiled at me crookedly. There was something so handsome and mischievous about the way he smiled.

"Oh, you don't have to do that. I'll be fine."

"Are you sure? Because you look frozen. And I can tell you're not drunk like your friends out there, so I thought you might need some warming up..." Ian said, sweetly.

The fact that those "friends" included his daughter and son didn't get past me.

"Okay. Hot chocolate sounds good actually."

Anything sounded better than going back out to the hot tub with those snots.

"Come on then. Let's make some." I followed Ian through the hallway and down another hallway that led to an industrial-sized kitchen.

"Sit." He pointed at a tall wooden stool by the counter. This is what people call a breakfast bar, I thought, stupidly. Perhaps that half bottle of alcohol had affected me more than I realized, my thoughts turning silly and strange.

The kitchen was huge, with double ovens and stainless-steel appliances that were so shiny I could almost believe that they'd never been used before.

"I hope I'm not getting your stool wet," I said, shifting around uncomfortably as I watched Ian opening and closing cabinets, looking for the hot chocolate I presumed.

"Oh, silly me! I'm so rude. Just a second."

I watched as Ian disappeared from the room, then I popped up from the stool and uselessly tried to dry the stool off with my too-damp towel.

"Don't worry about that," Ian said from behind me, and I jumped.

In his arms, Ian held a soft, creamy blanket. "You can put this on, and I'll take that."

I unwrapped the towel and handed it to him. He stood there, holding the blanket, and looking at my blue bikini. For the first time all night, I didn't feel ashamed or embarrassed.

I let him drink me in with his eyes.

"T-this will warm you up," Ian said, looking embarrassed as he handed over the blanket and turned back toward the cabinets.

I let the soft blanket consume me and I watched this handsome man, who was old enough to be my own father, as he poured me a mug of hot chocolate and topped it off with small, fluffy marshmallows.

I thought the conversation with Ian would be awkward, but he smiled warmly and drank his hot chocolate in silence. When we were done, he offered me another cup.

"You know, if those boys are bothering you or you feel uncomfortable, I'd be happy to take you home. Or you can just sit in the living room and watch TV, if you want. Don't let them pressure you into drinking. I know it's strange, letting my kids drink and all. But I'd rather they did it here safely than at someone else's house. Does that make sense?"

I nodded. When he explained it that way, it did sort of make sense.

"You seem like an interesting girl, Willow. Not the kind that likes to get drunk and act silly. Tell me what you do for fun," Ian said, blowing steam from the top of his mug.

And strangely enough, it didn't feel weird at all, telling this older stranger about my love for books and writing, my desires to become a schoolteacher someday.

As I sat there in Ian Ashcroft's expensive kitchen, with his warm blanket and kind parenting, I felt even more jealous of Chloe and Blake. It didn't seem fair that they got to have the perfect house and the perfect life … and also the perfect dad.

Chapter Nine

FAKE BODIES

CURRENT DAY

It's time to come clean about that summer.

I folded the note into a tiny square, tucked it in my back jean pocket, and climbed down from the loft, breathily.

That summer. I didn't know the author of the note, but I did know one thing for certain—"that summer" the note referred to had to be the summer Kathi Jo ran away.

As usual, my cell phone was getting zero bars. For a moment, I wondered how teenage-me would have felt about spending summers here, if I'd been a teenager during a different time—a time when cell phones were needed to socialize. To function.

I'm glad cell phones weren't around back then. But then again, maybe we would have felt safer and got in less trouble, if we'd had access to our parents and the rest of the world as easily as we do now.

I took the phone outside, holding it out in front of me as I zigzagged across the lawn, stepping around unused mulch bags and a row of lights and stepstones that I wasn't used to yet.

Still nothing.

I took a left at the end of the driveway, walking the lonely lane, holding my phone in the air. To my right were more woodlands; to my left, the lake. And, next door, was the empty lot where Kathi Jo's home once stood.

I know what you did.

Kathi Jo left because of me, but nobody else knew that. *No one except Kathi Jo...*

I stopped in front of the empty lot, pleased to discover that I now had two bars of service. As I dialed the number for the county sheriff's office, I surveyed the thick row of trees. Looking for watchers ... for the person who had planted that awful mannequin for me to find. The same person who left the note. *Could it be someone nearby ... someone within walking distance?* I wondered.

And what are their motives here? To get me to admit my secrets? To rattle me into leaving town?

Seeing the empty lot of Kathi Jo's home brought back memories of her mother. She didn't stay long after Kathi Jo disappeared … finally ditching Hillendale and going to live with relatives in another state. Was Isabella dead and gone now, like my own parents? Or was she still out there somewhere, missing her daughter and wondering what truly happened to her that summer on the lake?

I also thought about Kathi Jo's biological father, the one I'd never met. *Did he know about his missing daughter? Did someone track him down and tell him she was gone after it happened?* He never showed up in Hillendale to look for her. Did he search for her elsewhere, or did she turn up at his home again, interrupting his new family and new life? These were things I hadn't thought about in many years, but since returning to Hillendale, I'd had no choice but to revisit the days of my youth, and the awful loss of my best friend.

Her mother moved away, and her father didn't seem to care… Everyone in town, even her closest friends, seemed to accept that she had just ran away.

But then I reminded myself—*I assumed that too. I never searched for her either.*

"Sheriff's Office," the gruff voice on the other end of the line sounded just like Officer Spanos.

"Hi. My name is Willow Roberts. I own the lake house on 1 Daisy Lane."

"Yes. I remember. We met at your apartment last night," he said, briskly.

When I said nothing, he asked, "What can I do for you today?" *Oh, I don't know. Maybe you can explain to me why someone put a fake dummy in the closet of my lake house. A dummy that uncannily resembled my missing best friend from childhood!*

"Well," I dug the word out, exasperated, "I was hoping you could give me some sort of update."

I knew it was pointless. Surely, these small-town police officers in this tiny, backwater town knew next to nothing, just like they knew nothing all those summers ago when she ran away from Hillendale.

"Well, there is something," Officer Spanos said, proving me wrong. My mouth fell open in surprise.

"The dummy was no typical store-bought prop, Willow. It had a serial number on it," he said.

I clutched the phone tighter to my ear, adrenaline buzzing in my veins.

"If you know the serial number, you can trace the purchaser. Right?" I said, hopefully.

"Not sure on that quite yet," Officer Spanos huffed. He coughed loudly into the receiver, and I pulled the phone away from my ear for a second, flinching.

"So, where did it come from then?" I asked, voice

shaking with desperation. If this was some sort of "harmless" prank, I wanted to know that. Because if it wasn't that, then someone out there had more sinister intentions. And those intentions were probably directed at me. Perhaps this someone knew exactly what happened to Kathi Jo all those years ago when she vanished from town…

"Well, it seems to have come from an online vendor. A store that sells props and dummies for moviemakers and the like. And these fuckers look realistic, too. They'll customize them to order, design it however you want… They're not cheap."

My breath caught in my chest. "So, someone went to a lot of trouble to have it made. It took time and planning. Money. Have you contacted the company yet?" I asked.

Officer Spanos coughed again. "Look, Miss Roberts. I know you're concerned, but we're working on the details here. I'll update you as soon as we know more," he said, effectively telling me to butt out.

I groaned. "Okay. Can you at least tell me what this company is called? I'd like to look it up for myself." I was certain he'd refuse me, not wanting to tell me any more than he already had. But he surprised me when he said, "It's called designacorpse.com. Weird ass site, if you ask me. But I guess people are into that kind of thing."

"Thank you. And you'll let me know if you find out anything else?" I pressed.

"Sure will." He hung up before I could say goodbye.

WINTER '00

I spent most of the fall and early winter thinking about Lake Hillendale. The school days kept me busy, but at night, even communicating with Kathi Jo over phone and instant messenger, I felt cut off from my summertime friends.

"Blake took me to the theater in Greenville. They had these plushy red velvet seats and golden ropes. He bought me candy and popcorn..." Kathi Jo went on and on.

I twirled the phone cord around my finger, tucking my knees up to my chest on my twin-sized bed. My bedroom at the trailer had changed, just as Kathi Jo's room had last summer. The *Titanic* posters had been replaced with rock bands and quirky quotes, even though I still worshipped the movie. The small toys on my dresser had been switched out for make-up, scrunchies, and my cheap jewelry collection from Claire's.

"How was the movie you all went to see?" I asked. Although I didn't really care. I was growing bored with these nightly conversations, and tonight I was eager to hang up so I could get back to reading my murder mystery and eating my chips and dip, which was what I'd been doing before she called.

"Oh, you know. It was one of those shoot-em'-up sort of deals. Blake liked it, but it was a snooze-fest for me. Luckily, there was lots of snacks to keep me busy. And the make-out sessions, too." I could hear her smiling through the phone, and I couldn't help smiling myself.

As much as her relationship with Blake bored me, I liked knowing she was happy.

I missed her. And I missed summer. Not the drunken escapades at the fire tower or that lame-ass night at the hot tub where I drew more pleasure from talking to Blake's father than my own friends. And not the boats or the tanning or the water…

I missed the simple moments, moments when roasting the perfect marshmallow was as serious as science, and when we created our own mysteries from dust and mouse bones.

Kathi Jo was still talking, but I'd grown spacey, thinking about how far away summer was … but at the mention of Ian Ashcroft I sat up straighter on the bed.

"What did you say? Sorry, I blanked out there for a sec."

Kathi Jo sighed, as though repeating herself was an Olympic feat to overcome.

"They're getting a divorce. Blake's mom and dad. Blake's all bent out of shape about it."

"Oh. I wonder why," I said, casually.

"The real 'why' is why they stayed together in the first place. They live in separate worlds, and they're rarely home at the same time. If I had to guess, I'd assume they stayed together because of the money," Kathi Jo said.

"Hmmm."

"So, yeah ... he's upset about it, and he's been a real bummer to be around at school. He barely wanted to hang out during winter break after our movie date. I hope he's not seeing someone else," Kathi Jo said, nervously.

As much as it made me feel like a bad friend, I couldn't focus on Blake right now. There was something strangely satisfying, knowing that even rich, perfect-seeming parents can fight and split up too.

"So, who's going and who's staying? In the house, I mean..." I said, picking at my cuticles.

"Ian is leaving. He told Blake's mom that she could keep the place," Kathi Jo said. I could hear her on the other end, lips muffled and teeth working at what was probably a loose hangnail. She'd always had a terrible habit of biting her lip, and recently she had also started chewing on her fingernails and the ragged skin around her cuticles.

Damn. So, if Ian is leaving, I'll probably never see him again. He seemed so nice. Nicer than his son, I thought, sullenly.

Across from my bed there was a full-length mirror anchored to the wall. My hair was growing out, but it was stringy and greasy all the time. And I was starting to get acne.

Girls at school used expensive skin products, got highlights in their hair, and wore designer clothes. Most days, I couldn't help feeling like having more money would solve some of my cosmetic problems.

Kathi Jo was still blabbing in my ear about Blake's father.

"Ian works at the casino in Greenville. I'm pretty sure he's the big cheese over there. I think that's why they are so loaded. Your dad probably knows him pretty well. Didn't you tell me he has a gambling problem?"

I closed my eyes and took a deep breath. Sometimes, I regretted sharing all my secrets and personal info with my best friend. It often came back to bite me later.

Pretending I didn't hear her, I asked, "So, where will Ian go then? It doesn't seem fair that he should have to give up that big house on Lake Hillendale."

"He'll be fine. He rented a fancy loft in Radcliffe. That new one they built last year. Looks like a big metal space building, if you ask me. All that money and they can't get along. Crazy, right?" Kathi Jo said.

"Money isn't everything, I guess. My own mom and dad make me wonder sometimes... I don't know who would go and who would stay if they finally decided to call it quits."

"Oh, Willow. I'm sorry," Kathi Jo said, softly.

Dad was gone more and more often, and my mom seemed more depressed by the day. I'd heard some talk of money problems, late at night when they thought I was sleeping, and always in angry whispers and tones. Part of me wondered if we would even bother taking a family trip to the lake this year.

"It's okay," I said.

"Besides, it's not like anybody would fight over who got to keep the trailer, right?" Kathi Jo said, with a low chuckle.

I flinched. Kathi Jo came from a single-parent household. And I knew they weren't rolling in money either. But, somehow, since joining up with Blake and his pals, she had turned rather uppity, like them.

"Yeah. Probably not. Hey, I got to go. My mom is calling me for dinner," I lied.

Moments later, I put the phone on the hook and laid back on my bed. My murder mystery still lay open on the bed beside me, my page marked, but I was no longer interested in somebody else's story.

I flipped over on my belly and buried my face in my pillow. Like so many nights before, I imagined the pillow were a person beneath me. The soft cotton like the flush of lips on my cheeks and chest.

Turning over onto my back, I squeezed the pillow to my chest and wrapped my arms tightly around it, pretending it was someone who loved me lying on top of me, keeping me warm.

Chapter Ten

THE HEART OF LAKE HILLENDALE

CURRENT DAY

Despite the early morning chill, I stripped off my yellow sweater and sweats, all the way down to my bathing suit. The crew at the lake house were busy, getting back to work today—laying mulch in the backyard and doing minor repairs to the wooden planks on the porch at the front. Yet, I could feel them watching ... wondering what this crazy lady who paid their wages was thinking, swimming in Lake Hillendale mid-October.

I contemplated diving in; the thought of slicing through those familiar waters, graceful and swanlike, was appealing. But instead, I took the old familiar stairs, one, two, three ... and then I was underwater.

It was a strange feeling, being back in the lake. My thoughts were stranger still, wondering if the water remembered, if it recognized my body when I stepped inside it. For so long, I'd felt uncomfortable in my own skin. I'd like to say that things had changed in adulthood, but still, nothing fit, and I always felt self-conscious about my body.

This was not my body. I was just part of the lake, an extra tentacle of a great big octopus. I flipped onto my back and just floated. Rotating my shoulders and arms, I squinted up at the sun as my body skimmed across the surface of the lake. The water was cold, but I couldn't feel it anymore.

Kathi Jo was still gone, but at least I knew it wasn't her I found in the closet.

I should have been relieved, happy even … but there was a deep well of despair in my chest. I thought I might finally get answers. Closure. But now I felt more lost and confused than ever, and still unsure who had left the mannequin or the note for me to find.

As I rolled onto my stomach and turned for the shore, I saw several pairs of eyes watching me. Cindy down on her haunches with a bag of mulch, eyes following me in the water. And a couple other workers, pretending to work but watching me instead. And someone standing at the edge of the shore … hands shielding their eyes to block out the sun and see me better.

I swam toward her, doing breast strokes that burned my muscles but felt so good.

"Any news?" I pulled myself onto the muddy bank, shivering as my wet body connected with the icy cold morning air.

Officer Beckham was in full uniform. She looked like a little girl playing dress-up.

"Some," she said, giving nothing away. I followed her line of vision, the underwater stairs leading down.

"Those stairs are neat. Almost like…"

Don't say it.

"An underwater world … something from a fairytale," Officer Beckham said, her voice full of wonder

That's what we used to think, too, I thought, bitterly.

"I would have loved living here as a kid," she said.

"Yeah … I didn't live here though. We only visited in the summer. I never fit in, not fully," I said.

"I went to the school yesterday," Officer Beckham said, shifting gears. "I questioned all the students and staff. Tried to see if any of them knew Kathi Jo or might know something about the prank dummy."

"You questioned them all in one day? Wow, you're fast." I rested my bare foot on the first step in the water. There used to be two steps showing, but the water level had risen even higher since my youth.

"Well, it's a small school. Less than a hundred kids and staff," Officer Beckham said, defensively.

"Did any of them know anything?"

Officer Beckham shook her head. "Most of the staff were young, none remembered Kathi Jo. And none of the students had heard about her running away, but one of the kids mentioned something."

I looked up, hopeful. Could it have been a kid messing around ... leaving the mannequin and the note as a stupid pre-Halloween trick?

Officer Beckham shook her head. "It was nothing important, not really. Only that they dug up a time capsule in the school yard a few years ago. It's a tradition here, apparently. Every fifteen years, they unearth a box full of mementos, left behind in a time capsule by one of the younger classes. They dug one up from 2000."

My heart fluttered in my chest. The year 2000 didn't feel like twenty-two years ago. It didn't even feel like ten.

"Did Kathi Jo leave anything behind that year?" I asked.

"Just this. A kid's necklace. I don't think it's anything important though." Officer Beckham took out a small plastic bag from her pocket and handed it to me. My fingers were wet, hands shaking as I opened the bag and took out the necklace inside it.

It was a big, fake blue diamond in the shape of a

heart, surrounded by tiny, fake white diamonds on the border. I recognized it instantly. *The heart of the ocean.*

Tears flooded my eyes and I blinked rapidly, trying to keep them at bay. I dropped the necklace back in the bag, wiped my face, and handed it back to Officer Beckham.

"It's a cheap replica of the necklace from the movie *Titanic*. Rose's shitbag husband gives it to her in the movie, but she doesn't care about money or power... She loves the poor boy who she befriends on the boat. His name was Jack. At the end of the movie, old lady Rose throws the necklace back in the ocean, even though it was worth a fortune. She had lost the love of her life, so the necklace no longer mattered. The heart of the ocean, they called it..." I realized I was rambling and closed my mouth.

"Ah. Never seen the movie," Officer Beckham said, softly.

I shook my head and looked out over the water.

"It's nothing special, you know, these steps." I put both of my feet on the top step and swirled the water around in slow, ripply circles. "The houses around here are sinking, and the water level is rising. These steps are just a memory of what once was, nothing special about them. They are just sad, sad steps," I said, hypnotized by the water.

"That sucks. I like thinking of them as something magical... It's more fun that way," Officer Beckham said.

"Me too. But nothing stays the same forever. Someday this whole town will probably be underwater. Swallowed up by Lake Hillendale and lost forever … just like Kathi Jo was," I said.

SPRING '00

I found the necklace in a cheap jewelry store in Radcliffe, mixed in with movie posters and next to a bin of $5 CDs. I wanted to buy one of the CDs—Rage Against the Machine or Missy Elliot, I couldn't decide.

But if I bought a CD then I wouldn't be able to get the necklace. So, I put the music back and carried the necklace up to the counter. It only cost $4.

In truth, I wanted to keep it for myself, pretend I was Rose when I was all alone in my bedroom…

But I knew the necklace was perfect … a perfect gift for my best friend.

My summer trip to Lake Hillendale was still a couple months away, and I couldn't wait that long to give it to her. So, I wrapped the necklace in pink tissue paper and placed it carefully in an envelope, then I mailed it to Kathi Jo. Weeks later, I was still waiting for her call. I thought she'd be more excited about my gift. If she didn't want to wear it to school, then we could at least use it as a prop when we went out on the lake and did our role-playing.

Finally, I called and asked her myself.

"Did you get the necklace I sent you?"

"Oh yeah!" Kathi Jo sounded far away that day, her voice muffled on the other end of the line. I could picture her right then, sitting on her bed, phone tucked between her shoulder and chin as she painted her nails matte black or purple.

"Thanks for it. It looks like one of those things we used to get out of the bubble gum machine from the pizza place. Remember that?" Kathi Jo said.

Her words cut right to my core. Sure, it was cheap—only four bucks. But I'd spent the only four bucks I had to get her a gift. Did she even remember our favorite movie?

Before I could say anything else, I heard voices in the background. Blake, Tommy, and Trevor—telling her to hurry up. "Hey, Willow! I got to go. Blake's mom is driving us to the mall! Call me tomorrow, yeah?"

"Yeah, okay." I hung up, unsure why I felt so disappointed it. She had received the necklace and she said thank you. What more could I ask for?

Chapter Eleven

NEIGHBORHOOD FRIENDS

CURRENT DAY

I followed the old, familiar signs for Lake Hillendale into the center of town. Even though I'd already been back a month, I couldn't get used to the changes. The old food mart had been replaced with a trendy grocer, the mom-and-pop shops like the hardware store and family-owned pharmacy were gone. Besides the bait shop and a couple town staples, like the barber's and the movie theater, the town had evolved. There was a Starbucks and a small Kroger now, as well as other trendy shops and stops along the way.

I parallel parked my car between a jacked up black truck and a bright blue Jeep in front of a sandwich shop simply called "Sammy's". I'd eyed it a few times since coming to town but hadn't stopped to try it yet.

Most days, I kept to myself, using the foot bridge to travel back and forth to my apartment and the lake house, going into town for necessities only. My evenings were spent alone, watching television or reading. Eating those awful microwave dinners.

But today, I felt compelled to get away from the tainted lake house and the loneliness of my apartment. Someone knew I was in town, and someone was messing with me. But why? What was their motive? And who left that note for me to find? I once again wondered.

A bell rung as I entered the narrow restaurant. There was a tight open kitchen in the back, and rows of about twenty booths out front. I chose a booth in the far-left corner, next to the window but with my back to the wall. I needed privacy so I could research this designacorpse.com website for myself.

A pretty waitress with plaited braids and a name tag that read "Martine" brought me a menu and smiled shyly before walking away. Through the window, I watched a fleet of boats and trailers pass by, rowdy men playing music and drinking their beers behind the wheel.

It wasn't that unusual to see random rowdy people in Hillendale, especially in the summer season. Hillendale was a half local, half seasonal kind of town. The visitors brought in money, but they were also a nuisance.

At one time, my family was considered part of that "summer people" crowd; we were never real townsfolk, like Blake's, Tommy's, Trevor's, and Kathi Jo's families.

I ordered a Reuben, fries, and a Coke, then took out my phone. My stomach grumbled noisily as I typed in the website Officer Spanos had mentioned. Designacorpse.com. Just the mere thought of it made goosebumps break out on my arms and legs. Who comes up with that sort of thing? I wondered.

There were only a few other patrons in the restaurant, but I kept the phone close to my chest as the site sprang to life on my phone screen. Part of me had expected it not to even work when I typed in the address.

But my screen filled with images of dead people—not dead, but fake dead. Mannequins for sale. I clicked through them, one by one, looking for some sort of description. Some sort of explanation.

One page read: *Perfect for Halloween decorations!* next to a bloated, bloody corpse of a man that didn't look human at all, more like a zombie. *Okay, that sort of makes sense. People like to decorate. I get that.*

But other mannequins on the site were more realistic —these were suggested for movie props, or even crime scene enthusiasts who wanted to recreate crimes and conduct their own personal research. What sort of research are they doing on their own? I wondered.

I thought back to the old days with Kathi Jo … oh,

how our imaginations soared during those boring dog days of summer. We would have loved to have a prop like that, doing our own "crime scene analysis" like we did in the old days with chicken bones and animal carcasses.

The site was interesting. Strange, but perhaps not as strange as what I had expected.

What was really odd was the fact that someone had a mannequin specifically designed to look like Kathi Jo, and then they'd placed it in my home for me, specifically, to find. That was no coincidence. And it certainly wasn't a childish prank.

Someone wanted me to find it. They wanted me to react...

When I looked up, the waitress was coming towards me with a hot plate of food. I turned my phone over on the table and smiled as she set down my sandwich and fries in front of me. The food looked delicious. If it was as tasty as it looked and smelled, then it would probably be the best thing I'd eaten in months.

As I lifted my sandwich to take a bite, my eyes connected with a man on the other side of the restaurant. Seated alone in a booth, he was staring right at me, but he wasn't smiling.

I chewed my food so I wouldn't gasp; taking him in with my eyes as I struggled not to choke on the thick rye bread. It was hard to believe it but the man across the restaurant was my old friend Trevor.

Unlike Tommy, Trevor looked emaciated—thin and pallid, with a scraggly reddish-brown beard. I would have sworn he was ten years older than he was. He used to be on the heavier side, the smiley, outgoing one of the group. This man looked nothing like the former boy I'd known as a teenager.

Slowly, I lifted my hand and waved. But instead of waving back, he stood up. *Oh no, he's coming over here.*

I should have welcomed a chance to speak to him, an old friend, but like I'd done with most of the people in this town, I'd tried to forget him.

Plus, Trevor didn't look well. And I had a mouthful of bread and a website full of dead body lookalikes on my phone…

But instead of coming to my table, Trevor veered left and went out the door.

Well, that's strange.

Through my window seat, I watched him climb behind the wheel of the big black truck parked directly in front of my car. His engine roared to life, so loud it rattled the windows of the diner, and then he was gone.

I wondered if he was still friends with Tommy. He looked so different, disheveled and down-and-out. Not the happy-go-lucky, loud and pervy Trevor I remembered.

But were any of us happy-go-lucky after that final

summer? Probably not, I realized. It changed us. It changed Kathi Jo so much that she left for good.

They didn't know the woman I'd become since leaving Hillendale, and I certainly didn't know these people from my childhood anymore either.

I took a few more bites and picked at my fries, then gave up eating. My appetite was shot after seeing Trevor and those ghastly "corpses" online. Pushing my plate away, I picked up my phone and found a section on the website with customer service info. I typed up a quick email to their support service, then erased it.

Talking to a real-life person would probably get me farther than an email, I decided.

After paying my bill at the front register, I left a generous tip for the waitress. Outside, back in my car, I rolled my windows up and dialed the number.

I didn't expect anyone to answer, but the line was picked up immediately by a man on the other end. He rambled off two or three sentences about Design a Corpse and their current specials, then I told him my name and my address.

After a childhood of secrets, one thing that adulthood has taught me — telling the truth is usually your best option. So, I told the man on the other end about the body in my closet. That it resembled a friend of mine. That I was hoping he could give me some information about who might have sent it.

"1 Daisy Lane, you said?"

I sat up straighter in my seat, pulse pounding in my throat.

"Yes, that's the one," I told him.

"I'm sorry," the man said, "but we have a strict privacy policy here. I feel for you, ma'am, I do. But I can't give out the names of our customers." Perhaps, with a warrant, Tommy would be able to get the information we need, I thought hopefully.

"I understand, really. And I don't expect you to give out your customers' names. But here's the thing…" I took a breath and changed my mind—*sometimes lying is better*. "My sister is a prankster, or at least she used to be when we were kids. I'm sort of hoping that it came from her, you see … and if so, I'd like to buy one of those dummy things for myself so I can send one back in response. So, I guess what I'm asking is … I don't need to know the name of who bought it. I was just hoping you could tell me where it was sent from. Like, the state or town information … and that way, if it is her, I'll know it and I can return the favor." A forced chuckle escaped through my lips. Even to myself, this sounded far-fetched and desperate.

But if I knew the mannequin was sent from Hillendale, then I'd at least know the person who sent it was local. Or—a terrible thought split through my mind—*what if my ex-husband sent it? As some sort of warning?* That was something I hadn't considered until now.

But that made no sense; he didn't know about Kathi Jo. Not really. He knew I had a friend who ran away when I was younger, but I'd never mentioned her name. At least I didn't think I had...

The man on the other end of the phone said, "I don't know ... but listen. I'll take down your information and talk to my boss. If he says I can give you more info about where it came from, then I will. And if you do buy one of our corpses, can you please use my name—I'm Timothy —that way I can get the commission?"

I smiled despite myself. "If you can get me that information, Timothy, then I promise I will buy one from you."

SPRING '00

Summer break was only a couple short months away, but my thoughts about the lake were even farther. Hillendale may as well have been located on the other side of the world, for all I cared. My focus had shifted to Radcliffe.

It had a taken a couple cold months to hatch my plan —getting a job in the city of Radcliffe and saving up enough money to buy new clothes, jewelry, and possibly a car soon.

I'd reached out to every local business in the city that

was hiring minimum wage, underage workers. I'd received a few sympathetic nos and several rude ones, but then I'd reached Kandace at Mr. Sweet's Shop, a candy and nut bazaar—or so it fashioned itself. Kandace, or "Candy" as the regulars called her, needed a "pretty young girl" to run the register—her words, not mine.

The pay was shit and my ride situation wasn't secured, but I told Candy over the phone that I'd be in there at 4pm after school on the following Monday, as requested. The job wasn't a sure thing—I had to interview and "prove myself"—but I'd gotten this far and there was no way I'd let myself screw it up now.

"A job? Are you sure that's a good idea?" Mom asked. I'd heard plenty of parents insisting their young, work-age kids should join the workforce. I'd never heard of one discouraging the choice. But Mom never failed to surprise me.

"It's just, how will you get there? And what about school?" she asked.

She was right about the first part—the ride issue was a big one. But as far as school was concerned, Candy and I had already discussed that.

"I'll go in every day at four after school, and work until closing. Just on the weekdays. It won't interfere with school, I promise. Besides, my grades are good this semester." I wasn't lying; my grades were on point, the coursework this year easier than I'd expected. Sure, I'd have to study during my lunch break and do homework at night after work, but I'd manage. I needed this job. I needed something separate from home and Hillendale ... a path of my own.

"Okay," Mom said, drawing it out dramatically. "That's great, honey. But you know Dad and I don't get home until after five. How would you get there each day?"

I was old enough to get my permit now, and soon I'd be old enough to sit the license exam. Passing the test wasn't the problem; affording a car was. I knew Mom and Dad were struggling, and there was no way they would buy one for me. If there was any hope of owning a vehicle someday and driving down to Hillendale to hang out with my friends on the off-season, then I'd have to earn it myself.

"Having this job will allow me to save up. For my own car and maybe even college..." I pleaded.

"I know. And I think that's wonderful. But still, how will you make it there by four?" Mom asked.

I'd thought this through. I just didn't know if it would work. Sydney McCanelli lived in the trailer catty-corner to mom and dad. She was a loner, living by herself even though she was only nineteen or twenty. She looked rough around the edges, hair dyed black and blue, and kohl-rimmed eyes. Whenever I tried waving at her, she practically snarled at me.

But I knew that Sydney worked second shift at the laundromat on Pearl Street. Pearl Street was only a couple blocks away from Mr. Sweet's Shop. I just needed to get her to take me to Pearl Street; I'd walk the rest of the way myself. And hopefully hitch a ride back with her too.

"Sydney from across the street. She works nearby. I told her about the job, and she offered to let me ride in with her each day," I lied.

"Sydney. That weird girl with the jalopy and loud music?" Mom tugged on her earlobe, the way she always did when she thought I was lying.

"Yeah. She's not so bad, Mom. She lives alone and she's only, like, nineteen. I promised to give her some gas money each week. I think I would be the one helping her out, if I'm being honest..." It was a total lie. All of it was. I hadn't even asked Sydney yet. But I knew there was nothing my mom loved more than thinking she was important enough to give "charity" to those less fortunate.

"Okay. As long as you think it will help her ... and only if your dad says it's okay."

~

Later that night, my father said yes. Actually, it was more of a "humph"; I'm not even sure if he really heard my mother. The last piece to the puzzle involved walking over to Sydney's front door and knocking on it. I couldn't take no for answer. Not after getting this far.

But she said no right off the bat.

"I'm already late half the time, as is. I can't afford to lose my job, and taking you with me would be a nuisance. I don't like company anyway." Up close, Sydney was pretty. Beautiful even. Her eyes were dark brown, hollowed out with dark circles. With her porcelain skin, she looked like a gothic angel.

"You don't have to go out of your way for me at all. I'll just jump out at your work and walk the rest of the way to the shop. And if taking me home is an issue, my mom or dad can probably do that part."

"No."

I shifted from foot to foot, nervous. "I could pay you gas money."

"Not enough," Sydney said. She was leaning against the doorframe of her trailer. She looked bored. I tried to catch a glimpse past her into the living room beyond. I wondered what it would be like to live alone. It must feel lonely, but also cool and exciting. No one to tell me what to do, what to eat, when to go to bed…

"I'll give you a third of my paycheck every Friday until I get my own car. You said you couldn't afford to lose your job and you need the money, well, then, how can you turn down part-time work? All you have to do is let me ride in with you, and maybe home too … and it's like you're working part of my job too. I'll show you the check and give you your part every Friday. Deal?"

It was a stupid deal. I'd be lucky to clear a hundred and fifty bucks a week, and with Sydney's part, I might only make a hundred, or less. It would take forever to save up for a car this way, but it's not like I had any other options.

Sydney stepped back and let me inside. Stunned, it took me a minute to accept her invitation. Her trailer was smaller than ours, but cleaner. There was a worn-out sofa that looked like the kind with a bed hidden away inside it, and a small milk crate with an even smaller tv settled on top of it.

I could see through to her kitchen and dining area. They were sparse, but nice. The place looked bland compared to Sydney herself.

Sydney walked over the coffee table next to the sofa and reached for a pack of cigarettes.

I watched her pull one out, long and skinny like the ones Mom smoked sometimes, and light it with the click of a metal lighter.

"What's your real reason for taking this job? It's obviously not the money if you're willing to piss away a third of it on a ride." Sydney drew in a long puff, and then she smiled for the first time. She had odd teeth, small and pointy.

"Well, I do need the money. My parents can't afford to get me a car. And I need things. Clothes. Highlights…" I stared at the colorful strips of her hair.

"Ah. It's always about trying to impress someone else, right?" Sydney blew a smoke ring in my direction and smiled wider.

I wanted to correct her; I did. But there was nothing I wanted more than to roll into Hillendale with smooth, glossy skin, new clothes, and a decent, running, car.

"I guess you're right about that," I said, tucking my hands in my jeans' back pockets and waiting her out. *Please say yes*, I prayed inside my head.

"I'll do it. On one condition. Don't talk to me in the car. I like to meditate and listen to my music on the way. So, I'll pretend you're just not there. Oh. And the first time you try to rip me off and not pay me, the deal's off."

"I won't talk. I will pay. I promise." The words came out in a breathy rush of relief.

"Can you start taking me on Monday then?" I asked.

Sydney shrugged, then stubbed out her cigarette. "I guess. Now head on out. I got shit to do."

Chapter Twelve

SURPRISE VISITORS

CURRENT DAY

When I opened my eyes, Smokey's cold wet nose was pressed against mine. I blinked, smiling.

Scooting closer in the bed, I draped my arm gently over her fluffy body. She wasn't fond of being rubbed, except on the top of her head, so I treaded carefully when we were this close. She purred; eyes watchful as she bopped my nose again, gently with her own.

I'd never had a pet growing up. Unless you count the goldfish that I won at the country fair. I named her Goldie, big surprise. She came in a big glass bowl, and I found her upside down, belly up, in the bowl only a few weeks after bringing her home.

Jason wasn't fond of animals either. *They'll mess up the carpet or chew up our shoes*, he had warned.

I hated to get up and leave Smokey in bed alone, but I had to pee, and I wanted to check to see what time it was. The apartment was so dark and tomblike that it always felt like nighttime here.

I padded down the hall to the bathroom, shivering in my nightshirt and shorts. Smokey jumped down from the bed and followed at my heels, winding in and out between my legs, her thick fluffy tail swooshing against me. She watched me pee and then I carried her to the kitchen and fed her.

It was six thirty, the sun not up yet. Despite everything, I'd slept like a log last night.

I checked my phone for messages, from the police or the fake-corpse dealer. I'm not sure what I expected. They didn't call last night, and certainly they wouldn't call me this early in the morning either.

At the stove top, I mixed oatmeal and buttered a slice of bread. I hadn't invested in a toaster yet. Truthfully, I hadn't planned on staying in Hillendale long enough to need one.

After sitting down to eat, I shot off a text to the only person I knew would be up this early—Sydney. Of all my old friends, she was one of the few I stayed in touch with. Sydney had a husband now, and two baby twin girls. She was nothing like the girl she once was. She still lived in Branton, but she'd left the trailer park long ago, graduating to a three-bedroom home in the middle of suburbia with her double stroller and pack'n'plays.

Miss you, I texted. *How are the babes?*

Sydney started writing back immediately, three wiggly bubbles on my screen. That was one thing about Sydney—I could rely on her to be consistent. She was one of the only people who attended my father's funeral, and then also my mother's.

They are great. BUT HOW ARE YOU? Are you still in that awful town???!!! she texted back.

Sydney didn't approve of my return to Hillendale. *SELL THE FUCKING PLACE AND LEAVE THOSE MEMORIES BEHIND,* she scream-texted. I couldn't help smiling—mommy or not, Sydney still cussed like a sailor and snuck cigarettes every chance she got on her back porch. And she was never afraid to tell me what she thought, even if I didn't really want to hear it.

I started typing, telling her about what had happened, the body-not-a-body I'd discovered at my family's lake home. But I stopped. If I told Sydney the truth, she would really push for me to leave. And now that I was here, Kathi Jo's memory rushing back at me like a speeding train, I couldn't up and leave Hillendale. Not yet anyway.

I know. I'm going to leave as soon as renovations are over… I wrote back, finally.

I turned my phone over and chewed on my oatmeal. The oats tasted sour and felt mushy in my mouth. Probably expired. I needed to take a trip into town to get some food today and stop by the lake house again to check things out.

I put my bowl in the sink and bent down to rub Smokey's head. At the same time, we heard a thump below our feet. Smokey took off running, probably to go and hide under the bed again. For a cat ... she certainly acted like a scared little chicken, sometimes.

I stood, listening. The building was old, the pipes groaning from time to time. But then I heard another thump, followed by a low cough downstairs.

My heart raced. *Was someone down in the store? Had someone broken in?* The bait shop was closed up for the fall and winter, not set to open again until spring.

I opened the front door of my apartment and tried to peer below, through the metal grates of the stairs. I couldn't see or hear anyone. But in the parking lot, there was a blue pickup, parked a few spots over from mine.

I climbed down the stairs, slowly, and peered in the shop window below.

A man's face, old and bald, popped right up on the other side to look back at me.

"Jesus!" I took a small leap backward and clutched my chest.

"No, not Jesus. Just me." Bart, the shop owner, held the door to the shop open, motioning me to come inside.

"What are you doing here, Bart?" I didn't want to sound rude or ungrateful; after all, he was letting me stay in the upstairs apartment for a cheap price.

"Come help me. These are heavy." Bart bent at the waist and lifted a heavy cardboard box. He slammed it into my arms. He was right—it was heavy—and the way it rattled in my arms, I knew it was filled with bottles.

"Ran out of booze. Needed to borrow some from the shop to get me through the winter," he huffed.

"Ah." I watched Bart lift another heavy container and followed him out to his truck carrying mine.

He dropped the tail gate, and we slid the boxes in the back, grunting and groaning.

"Are you okay?" Bart slammed the tail gate shut and turned to me, hands resting on his narrow hips. He was old, nearly eighty now or close to it.

"Oh, everything is fine. The apartment is great and Smokey's a doll. All is well and good here, no worries," I said. I hoped he wasn't here to raise the rent, or worse, to tell me I could no longer stay in the apartment.

"That's not what I meant. How are you after what you found? I may be old, but I got ears and I got Facebook … and I heard that someone put a fake dummy of Kathi Jo in your parents' old place."

I was surprised he remembered her name so easily and that he had already heard about what happened.

When Kathi Jo disappeared, the local police dragged the lake and a few people put up fliers. But the general consensus was that she'd ran away. After all, she'd left a note behind.

I couldn't remember much about Bart from back then... *Did he help with the search efforts for Kathi Jo?*

"I'm fine. Any idea who would leave that mannequin for me, Bart?" I asked.

Bart had worked at the bait shop in Hillendale for as long as I could remember. If anyone knew the townspeople here, it was him.

"No clue. I always worried about her though." Bart scratched his head and turned away from me, his expression strangely emotional.

"How come?" I pressed.

"Her daddy was a real prick. I knew them both, her mom and dad, before she was born. A rough guy. He sold drugs to out-of-towners and liked picking fights. Although I was heartbroken for her and her mama when he skipped town, I don't think any of us really missed him. Or that loud motorcycle of his," Bart said.

I hadn't thought about Kathi Jo's absent father much until recently. I'd seen pictures of him in the past, but that was all.

"Kathi Jo would come waltzing in here with all those boys, in those skimpy outfits and those hoodlum piercings she wore. I was always telling her she should cover up her breasts or find new friends. I cared about her, you know? I still saw a little girl when I looked at her…" Bart rattled on.

There was a sour taste in my mouth. I didn't like the way he referred to her body or attire, as though her leaving town that summer might have been caused by something that was her own fault.

"I have to get going, Bart. I'm headed to the lake house today to get some work done." As he waved goodbye, I took a long, hard look at Bart. He seemed like a normal old man, but who knows? *It wouldn't be the first time an adult in this town took an inappropriate interest in an underage girl.*

~

In the light of day, the lake house looked almost homey. Welcoming.

The house was one of fifteen on this side of the lake. Most were empty this time of year.

Renovations were moving again, but the crew was gone for the day. I let myself in through the front door and took a deep breath. *Please no fake bodies or notes this time.*

I hadn't heard back from the corpse seller, and I wondered if I ever would.

Like the night before, I wandered through the downstairs bedrooms, making sure nothing was afoot.

My bladder was near its bursting point, so I headed for the bathroom, praying there was toilet paper left behind by the crew. This place didn't feel like home anymore, not really. Just a shell of the house it once was. I flipped on the bathroom light, closing the door behind me. Only one bulb was working. I sighed with relief when I saw the toilet paper hooked on the holder.

My pants were down around my ankles when I heard the noise. A soft creak, then another, just overhead.

I didn't check the upstairs loft, I realized in horror.

I stood, tugging on my jeans, and listened.

For a moment, I thought it was all a mistake … just the normal shifting and groans of an old lake house. But then I heard the steady thump of someone coming down the steps. My instinct was to lock the bathroom door and hide, but instead I stepped up to the door and shouted through it, "Who's out there?"

Please, be one of the workers…

But suddenly, the intruder was running, the sound of heavy boots thudding through the house and snapping my whole body tight with fear.

Impulsively, I flung the bathroom door open, just in time to see a hooded figure running out of the house, through the front door. I yelped in fear and shock, then moved to the open door and peeked out. The intruder was gone, but I could hear the distant roar of a vehicle coming to life. It sounded a whole lot like the truck I'd heard the other day at the diner, the one driven by Trevor.

Breathless, I closed the front door and locked it, then went around to check the back one too. *I'd obviously scared them off, but why? What were they doing in the house?*

SPRING '00

The job at Mr. Sweet's Shop was harder than expected. The buttons on the register were complicated and there was a lot of clean-up involved, especially at the end of my shift. But within a couple of weeks, I was working the register like a pro, a smile plastered across my face as I greeted each customer.

As much as I hated to admit it, I sort of enjoyed the work. The five hours I worked flew by, and I liked the two other girls who worked with me—Emily on Mondays and Wednesdays and Kianna on Tuesdays and Thursdays. Candy, the manager, was rarely there except on Fridays, so we goofed off some, and tried to make the best of our shifts.

Sydney worked at the laundromat until eleven, which meant I had two hours of downtime each night at the end of my shift while I waited for her to get off work and ride me back home. My parents weren't crazy about the idea, me rolling in at midnight on a school night. But I'd reminded them that I was almost an adult, and if they really wanted to pick me up from work themselves, they could. They had declined.

At nine o'clock, I clocked out and said goodbye to Kianna. Sometimes the two of us hung around and chatted for a bit, which helped pass the time. But most nights, her parents were outside waiting, and I was left behind on my own.

So, when the lights to the shop dimmed and the parking lot grew empty, I took the crosswalk to Merrill Boulevard and cut through the alleyway over to Main Street. Blake's father, Ian Ashcroft, lived in a building on Main Street. Every time I passed by it, I thought about that night with the hot chocolate, him chatting with me like an episode of *Full House* starring Bob Saget.

Ian's apartment building was tall and bright, a twisted hulking monstrosity that looked like it was trying too hard to be called swanky.

There was a gruff security guard and a gate in front of the parking garage, and two haughty doormen at the front and back of the building. Basically, there was no way in without an invitation. Instead, I waited and prowled, like a spider on Main Street, hoping I might catch Ian coming or going, in from the garage or waltzing up the street after a late dinner.

But after two weeks of nightly stalking, I failed to spot him or anyone familiar. I had, however, discovered a yummy pizza place next door. I spent half of my week's pay right there in that shop those first couple weeks, ordering greasy calzones and barbecue bacon pizzas with crunchy garlic toast on the side.

My lucky break came from no other than my best friend. I had told Kathi Jo about my new job at Mr. Sweet's Shop, and one Wednesday evening, thirty minutes before closing time, she waltzed through the double doors of the shop. Blake, Tommy, and Trevor were with her. Her own little entourage.

My face lit up like a Christmas tree when I saw them.

"I can't believe you guys are here!" I ran around the counter, untying my embarrassing brown apron. I hugged Kathi Jo. Even though we talked several times a week, on the phone or online, I hadn't seen her face since last summer. She looked prettier than I'd ever seen her. Her hair looked lighter, the dark hair dye fading out from the constant sun in Hillendale. Her hair was longer too; it hung down her back, cascading in waves.

The boys looked the same. Acted the same, too. They seemed stupid and loud, and they smelled drunk.

"We're on our way to see Blake's dad. Did you know

he lives right over there?" Kathi Jo jabbed a thumb in the direction of Main Street.

"Oh yeah. I forgot he moved out here," I said, nonchalantly, surprised she didn't remember telling me months ago.

Emily was working tonight. I introduced her to my friends, proud that I had so many.

"Emily. Such a pretty name." Trevor lifted her hand to his lips and kissed it.

I groaned. *What a turd.*

"If you guys wait, like, thirty minutes, I'll go with you. I have time to kill before catching my ride anyway." I directed this at Kathi Jo.

"Sure," Kathi Jo said. She strolled around the shop, looking in the cases. Then Trevor asked us to hook them all up with some free candy, as though they didn't have wads of cash in their pockets from their fancy allowances. Emily shot me a worried look.

"Don't worry," I told her, scooping sour cherry balls and cinnamon hard candy into baggies for my friends. "I'll pay for it myself when they leave." She nodded.

"I got it," Tommy said, giving me an apologetic smile. He handed two twenties to Emily, nearly double the cost of the candy.

My body was buzzing as I left work, the thrill of having my summer friends here with me in the city.

The night air was drizzly and unseasonably cool.

Kathi Jo lent me her jacket—this gaudy, pink thing that felt thin but looked like it was made of sheepskin. I zipped it up to my chin and took Kathi Jo's arm in mine. We skipped across the cross walk and emerged onto Main Street.

Blake had a key card to get in the building. *Must be nice.*

"Do you visit your dad here often?" I said, saddling up next to Blake.

"Yeah. Mostly weekends. Chloe hasn't come much though. She's sort of pissed at him over Mom."

"Oh." It made sense, I supposed. Kids choosing sides. *I wonder whose side I would take if Mom and Dad split*, I wondered. *Neither*'s, I decided.

Inside, we were met with a long hallway, each side lined with apartment doors. Each door was metallic and retro-looking, again, with the try-hard swank.

"He's upstairs." Blake led the way up a corkscrew staircase made of shiny metal, then at the top, he kept going to a third and fourth set of steps. Everything in the building seemed hard and wiry, jutting out at strange angles, giving me pseudo-Frank Lloyd Wright vibes.

"You sure he won't care if we pop in?" I said, breathless as we reached the fourth floor and stopped.

Blake rolled his eyes. "I don't think my dad will mind if I pop in. He's my dad," he said, defensively. I flushed. Blake could really be an asshole sometimes. And he seemed more possessive with Kathi Jo than I remembered from last summer; clutching her arm every chance he got and bossing her around in a way that made me feel uncomfortable.

Once inside the building, Blake used another key card to enter his dad's apartment. Following the others, I was taken aback by the huge open space. It wasn't what I had expected. The walls were painted in vibrant colors, floor to ceiling shelves lined with hard leather books in nearly every corner.

And the furniture, it didn't look fancy, but rather well-loved. A soft brown leather sofa with a colorful Afghan thrown over the back. A paint-chipped coffee table covered in candles and weathered paperbacks.

I slipped my holey sneakers off at the entrance.

"There's my boy!" Ian Ashcroft emerged from the shadows of a dark hallway, his hair wet and shiny from the shower. He had on a soft white t-shirt and jeans that fit nicely on his sinewy form; a thick towel was draped around his neck.

He looked younger and happier than I remembered. Definitely more handsome than Bob Saget.

"What's up, Dad?" Blake said.

"Let me fetch you all something to drink. I only have tea and Coke, hope that's all right." His eyes passed right over me; if he recognized me from that night when we talked last summer, he didn't show it.

I felt a rush of disappointment, and a burning sense of shame. Am I that forgettable?

Head down, I gathered with my friends in the kitchen. When Ian offered me a drink, I declined. My thoughts drifted back to that sweltering summer night when I was wet and freezing; Ian rubbing his hands on my back to warm me up, holding out that mug of hot chocolate. He had seemed so kind and interested in talking to me. *I guess he's a phony just like his son*, I thought, filled with disappointment.

I tried to listen and follow along with the conversations. Blake and his dad stood at the kitchen counter, discussing a local soccer team, and Trevor and Tommy bragged about their football stats.

"Let's go sit on the sofa. I'm sleepy," Kathi Jo said, nudging me. I let her lead me to the sofa. I felt myself sink into it. If I could have, I would have let it swallow me whole. Even though I was happy to see my friends, I felt this distance between us. Like they were all great friends, and I was just a hanger-on they saw every once in a while.

Ian's apartment was freezing, the jacket I'd borrowed from Kathi Jo too thin and worn for the arctic AC temperature inside. I wished, more than anything, to be home in my bed with a Patricia Cornwell crime novel and my heavy weighted blanket draped over me. Maybe a bag of candy from Mr. Sweet's, too. I still had some candy I'd bought tucked away in my dresser, and since taking the job, I'd already gained ten whole pounds. *So much for using my paychecks to improve my appearance*, I thought, drearily.

"Tell me about your new job and school," Kathi Jo purred in my ear, leaning her head on my shoulder. She smelled good, like Bath and Body Work's Plumeria lotion, our favorite, and Secret brand deodorant.

So, I did. I stroked my best friend's hair and told her all about Mr. Sweet's Shop and my new friends Emily and Kianna.

"Do I need to be jealous?" Kathi Jo teased.

"Of course not," I laughed.

A few minutes later, as I talked about the register and the sometimes rude customers, I watched, from the corner of my eye, as Ian excused himself to his office. The door to his office closed with a soft thud.

"I need to head back soon," I said, looking at my watch. It was a stupid Mickey Mouse wristband, the faux leather band falling apart, coming unraveled. "My ride will be getting off work in, like, thirty minutes." I wondered if Sydney would wait for me if I was late showing up at the laundromat. I seriously doubted it.

"Blake's staying the night here with his dad. But I'll walk you back. Or, if you want, you can ride back with me and the guys. Tommy has his license now too," Kathi Jo said.

"I don't mind taking you back," Tommy said, giving me a soft smile.

"Yeah, that'd be great," I said. I should have been happy, getting a chance to ride home with my bestie, to catch up with her and our friends. But I couldn't shake off my insecurities. *Even Ian's dad has forgotten who I am since last summer...*

Moments later, we were out on the street and back at Tommy's cute powder blue Volvo in the parking lot next to Mr. Sweet's.

On the way home, we stopped over at the laundromat so I could run in and tell Sydney I didn't need a ride.

"Whatever," she said, shrugging into her black leather jacket and climbing into her beat-up truck. "Suit yourself." She seemed almost hurt by it, refusing to even look over at my friends, who she probably viewed as rich and snotty.

The ride home was a blur, answering Kathi Jo's questions, asking the right questions back. I couldn't shake off this sinking feeling of disappointment and distancing from my former self.

~

But on the following Monday, Ian Ashcroft proved me wrong. He did remember me.

When Ian walked into the shop, I was stunned to see

him. I could barely get the words out to say hello, and my hands were shaking as he approached the counter.

"I heard you say you were working here now. I'm new in town and haven't had a chance to visit this place yet. Although, I don't know why not, because I've always had a sweet tooth."

"What can I get you?" It was such a canned response, but I couldn't manage to come up with anything better. My hair was pulled back in a tight ponytail, unwashed since Saturday. And the only make-up I'd worn tonight was the concealer to cover up the budding zit on my forehead.

"What's your favorite?" Ian was watching me intensely, that same crooked smile as before.

Unlike the other night when he barely seemed to know who I was, now he suddenly seemed aware only of me. Like I was the single thing in the room. The only girl in the universe, like that night at his fancy house when the others were drunk.

"I like the gummy bears," I said.

"The small ones or the big ones?" Ian asked, eyes never leaving mine. His gaze was so intense; I felt like I was on fire, under his microscope, every time he looked at me.

"The big ones," I said, pointing into the plastic case. "The ones that taste like cinnamon."

"I'll take a pound of those then," he said, smiling. I

busied myself, scooping the candies, weighing them, then wrapping them in a plastic bag.

When I rang him up for the gummies, he handed them over to me. "For you, Willow. Sweets for the sweet."

It was stupid and cheesy, but I blushed anyway, my stomach swirling.

"I thought you said you had a sweet tooth," I said, clutching the bag of bears to my chest.

"I do, but I haven't eaten any real food all day. Would you like to have dinner after work? I bet you get hungry while working. There's this amazing pizza place next to my apartment..."

Chapter Thirteen

PURSUIT

CURRENT DAY

"Are you sure you didn't see their face?" Tommy hovered over me. I was sitting, knees tucked protectively to my chest, body still shivering with anger and fear.

"No. Nothing. All I saw was their backside. They were wearing a dark hoodie and it was pulled up over their head. I couldn't even see their hair!" I exclaimed.

Despite feeling a brief sense of calm and relief right after the break-in, my fear was trickling back in. I couldn't stop my hands from shaking. I wrapped them around my knees and tried to breathe in through my mouth and out through my nose, like a therapist had once told me to do.

"Were they skinny or fat? Short? Tall?" Detective Beckham sat down on the stoop beside me. I knew she was trying to be comforting, but she felt too close. In fact, I regretted dialing 911 in the first place.

"Sort of tall, I guess. And in-between. Not skinny or heavy… All I know is that it has to be the same person who planted the dummy in my closet and…"

"And?" Tommy said, coming to stand over me. From where I was sitting, he looked like a giant. I shivered.

"And nothing. That's it. It has to be one and the same," I said, thinking about the note. There was no reason for me to keep the note to myself, but then again, it seemed to indicate I held some sort of blame for Kathi Jo's disappearance. The more I thought about it, the more I felt certain—*Kathi Jo didn't just get upset with me and skip town all those years ago. Something else happened. And someone nearby knows exactly what that something is.*

The note was still in my pocket, curled into a tiny ball. Showing them would have been the right thing to do, but it felt personal, meant just for me.

"I agree. It's probable that it was the same person who left the mannequin. Unless we have two people making mischief…" Tommy wondered aloud, glancing over at Officer Beckham.

"Oh, there was a truck! A loud one. I heard it in the distance, right after they ran away," I said.

"Good, that's something," Officer Beckham said, pulling out a small notepad. Again, I thought about Kathi Jo … those silly made-up scenarios we created with our own minds. *This sort of prank felt like something she would do; but that's a ridiculous thought,* I chastised myself.

I looked up at Tommy; the sun cast a glare over his features, and for a moment, he looked like the boy he used to be. For the life of me, I still couldn't reconcile the boy with the man. He had always seemed more responsible than the others, and kinder to me too. But he had been wild and impulsive back then … we all were. And looking at him now, in his proper police uniform with his hands on his hips and his official-looking hat, it felt like something out of *The Twilight Zone*.

One day you're just a kid and then—blink. You're middle aged and everyone around you is too.

But Tommy wasn't the only childhood friend who had changed. *Trevor.*

"I saw Trevor at the diner in town the other day. He didn't look good, Tommy. And I know he drives a big, loud truck, too."

But Tommy was already shaking his head back and forth. "Look, Trevor has had some problems, okay? His wife and kid left him a couple of years ago and he dabbles in drugs. I've had to pick him up and take him to the station a few times."

"So?"

"So, that doesn't mean he's the one doing this. He wouldn't. We were all friends then. Plus, he has no reason to bother you or stir up the past, Willow," Tommy said.

But I couldn't help thinking about that look on Trevor's face, that deadpan expression in the diner. He wasn't the smiling, joking, wild boy from my past. He had looked like a stranger, and one who wasn't very happy to see me back in Hillendale.

SPRING '00

So, that's how it started. A few nights a week, Ian and I met up at the pizza parlor by his house. He always paid for my dinner.

He always asked me about school and work. He was concerned for my safety, hanging around the sweet shop waiting for Sydney to get off work.

"I feel better when you hang out with me. At least I know you're safe. I still can't believe your mom and dad don't come pick you up."

Part of it felt like a betrayal—talking badly about my own parents with another parental figure. But the more time I spent with Ian, the more I realized how lucky Blake and Chloe were to have such a kind, involved, and interested father in their lives.

The first few meetups with Ian were a blur, me spouting off too-fast, too nervously … cheeks blustery with anxiety. But then, we settled into a gentle back-and-forth that started to feel more comfortable. Eventually, the conversation drifted from my life to his.

"I was sorry to hear about the divorce," I said, one night. I used a fork to cut the end off my slice of cheese pizza, delicately lifting the piece to my mouth. I'd learned that if I used a fork and ate slower, I could save myself a little bit of embarrassment. When I ate at my usual pace, I always ended up with fresh stains on my shirt and chin.

Ian waved me away. "No need to be sorry. It was over before it'd even started."

"What do you mean?" I had no idea how long the Ashcrofts had been married, but long enough to have children together so it had to mean something to them both.

"Joan and I were more friends than anything. Business partners in the casino, too. We got along and had similar interests, and when the kids came along, we had a stake in keeping our family together," Ian explained.

I couldn't help thinking of my own parents. Did they stay together only for my sake too, like business associates, the way Ian described his own marriage to Joan? I wondered.

"What happened between you then?" I asked, curiously. It was a mystery to me—why some people stayed together, and others didn't, even when it was clearly not working anymore. It seemed like a miserable existence to me.

"The kids grew up." Ian smiled, a touch of sadness in his tone. "They're practically adults now. Blake and Chloe are nearly there ... and they don't need us to keep up the façade anymore. I want Joan to be happy. Despite what she did, I still wish the best for her."

There was something pleasurable about hearing him calling his children "adults". Blake and Chloe weren't much older than I was; if he considered them adults, then maybe he considered me one too. I sat up straighter in my chair.

"You said 'despite what she did'. What did she do? If you don't mind me asking." Frustrated with the fork, I picked up the greasy slice of pizza with my hands and took several large bites. The bubbling hot cheese burned the roof of my mouth.

Ian leaned in, elbows on the table, and wiped the corner of my lip with his napkin. I froze, unsure how to react to this gentle gesture that almost felt fatherly in nature. My own parents were rarely affectionate, and I couldn't even remember the last time my father had hugged me.

"She cheated on me," he said, balling up the napkin

in his fist. He leaned back in his seat and shrugged, as though he couldn't care less about it.

"Cheated? Any woman who would cheat on you must be crazy." The words slipped out before I could stop them. "Sorry, but it's true," I added, staring into the doughy crater I was making on my pizza with the fork. Ian seemed like the perfect father and surely, that meant he was a good husband, too. Certainly not deserving of being cheated on.

Ian reached over again, using the tip of his finger to lift my chin. I stared into his eyes, and he stared back. They were like deep grey pools. Pools I could get lost in forever.

"Do you want to come over to my apartment tonight? We could watch a movie. Pop some popcorn," he offered.

My stomach flipped. "I'd love to, but I have to be back in less than an hour to meet my ride."

Ian frowned. I hated disappointing him but going to his apartment alone with him felt a little strange.

"I'm sorry," I added. "Maybe another time…"

"Okay. Or"—he held up one finger—"I have another idea." He leaned closer, lowering his voice conspiratorially. "Why don't you tell your friend Sydney that you already have a ride home? And then you can tell your parents that you're staying with friends?"

I considered this. Lying to my parents was a bad idea

and, although Sydney probably wouldn't mind, I didn't want her to stop offering me rides home in the future.

"But where would I actually stay? I don't get it."

Ian's smile grew wider, his teeth gleaming in the low lit restaurant. It made me nervous, but also a little excited. I took a deep breath, then told him yes.

Chapter Fourteen

THE RETURN

CURRENT DAY

A ny plans I had for that day ended the moment I woke up. I woke to my head pounding, throbbing in my ears... I wasn't much of a drinker, but last night I'd been so stressed and unable to sleep, that I'd cracked open a bottle of tequila that Bart had left in one of the cabinets over the stove.

Ten shots later, I was stumbling through the apartment, checking every narrow nook and cranny for intruders or notes. Checking through the blinds and curtains for shadows in the parking lot outside...

"Ugh." I brushed my teeth and downed two Advil. Yesterday I had promised myself that I'd follow up with Mack and the rest of the crew about the renovations. I didn't want to halt them again, but I couldn't put the crew in danger either. If someone was hanging out around the house, hiding fake bodies and making mischief ... they needed to know about it.

Somebody doesn't want me here in Hillendale. The sooner the renovations were complete, the sooner I could get the hell out of Dodge ... but I couldn't lie to Mack. They needed to be on guard.

I lay down on my sofa, nursing my head, and took out my cell phone. *I was ready to sell the lake house and go. I didn't know where I'd go—not back home either—but away from this hellish town that didn't want me when I was a kid, and sure as hell doesn't want me now.*

As I stared at my phone screen, I noticed the flash of a notification—a voicemail from an unknown number. I closed my eyes and dialed voicemail, praying my stalker hadn't graduated from creepy written notes and fake bodies to ominous voice messages...

I sat up in surprise when the message started.

"Hello there, Miss! We spoke the other day about you buying one of our personally designed corpse mannequins. I talked to my boss, and I was right about what I said ... we can't give out customer information. However, I do know that the particular model you received came from Greenville, Kentucky. Not sure if that helps you or not. Please give me a ring back as soon as you get this! I would love to share some of our latest deals with you over the phone… Let's chat about it…"

I clicked the phone off and gripped the phone tightly to my chest.

As suspected, the mannequin was purchased from someone here locally, someone close to Lake Hillendale.

SUMMER '00

I'd settled into a routine now—school all day and work all evening. With summer right around the corner, one might expect that I was dreading a return trip to Hillendale.

In fact, I was actually looking forward to summer at the lake house. I wanted to swim and sleep, see Kathi Jo … and I wanted to forget all about Ian Ashcroft.

At first, he had seemed like a sweet guy. He rented movies I'd never seen before—*Ghost, Mission: Impossible, Schindler's List*. I didn't have the heart to tell him that I preferred comedy movies. He had offered me a glass of wine, which felt wildly inappropriate, but not that shocking, really, since I knew that he allowed his own children to drink.

But then, one night, after a few too many drinks of his own, he tried to make a pass at me. It shouldn't have shocked me, but it did. All this time, I had enjoyed his company—enjoyed being treated like an adult. But I hadn't expected that from him.

It gave me mixed emotions, and most of them weren't good.

Ian was almost thirty-five years older than me. By the time I graduated from college, he might be eligible for senior citizen benefits.

The thought of it made me nauseous.

But there were other times when I wanted it. I wanted to give in and let him … let him grant me the experience of so many new things … let him touch me in places I'd never been touched before.

But I'd wanted a father figure, not someone to take advantage of me. And, although I was young, I wasn't naïve. I knew it wasn't normal. And that's why I had to stop seeing Ian.

I left the job at the candy shoppe, telling my boss that I'd soon be leaving for the summer with my family—which was true, but I left the job earlier than necessary in order to avoid Ian.

Candy had agreed to hold my position for me until August 25th, the week I returned to school. She had taken a liking to me, calling me a "one-of-a-kind worker" who always showed up on time and never called in sick.

I wasn't sure if I wanted to return to the job at all.

I needed a chance to get back to myself, my writing and my friends … my family.

Sydney was waiting for me in her truck that last night when I'd put in my notice to Candy, even though it wasn't eleven yet. She had her windows down and the AC blasting. I climbed in and shivered, then reached for my seatbelt.

"So, are we ever going to talk about it?" Sydney said, giving me a sidelong glance.

"Talk about what?" I snapped my belt in place and tucked my legs up in the seat, the way I had a habit of doing.

"That man you've been seeing. He's the real reason you're quitting, isn't it?"

"I'm not seeing him. He's a friend of the family," I lied. "And so what? It's over now. You haven't said a word these last couple months, and now you care all of a sudden?"

Sydney shot me a knowing look.

"Look, I'm sorry. I followed you a couple times," Sydney admitted.

"You what?" I was so stunned. Here was this girl, with her give-no-fucks demeanor and shitty attitude, and now she wanted me to believe she was worried about me?!

Sydney sighed. Her hands shook as she dug around in her coat pocket for her cigarettes.

"They're right here." I snatched the pack off the dash and held them out of her reach.

"Fine." Sydney frowned. "I was concerned about you. Especially the walking at night on your own. I was worried you were turning into a street hooker or something!"

I felt a sudden urge to crush the pack in my hands and toss it out the window.

"I was relieved when I pulled up and saw you with him. I figured he was your dad or something. Maybe an uncle ... but then I saw the way he looked at you. And watched you follow him up to his apartment. He's such a creep, Willow."

"Takes one to know one! Look at you, practically stalking me! And it sounds like you followed me more than once or twice."

"I'm sorry," Sydney said. She reached over and snatched the pack out of my hands. I sat quietly, with my hands in my lap, as she slid a cigarette out and put it between her lips.

"Don't be sorry. Just drive me home, please. It's a good thing you won't have to drive me to work anymore, or follow me around town, stalking me." I looked out the passenger window, at the city lights and the spire of Ian's dark building in the distance. I hadn't given myself enough free time to really feel it. How bad it hurt to be betrayed by him, by everyone. My friends, my family, other adults ... even Sydney. Sometimes, it felt like no one was really on my side. They all had their own problems or agendas.

"You ever wonder why I live alone and I'm only eighteen?"

I turned my head to look at her. "I thought you said you were nineteen."

Sydney shrugged. "I lied."

"Okay. Eighteen, nineteen … you're an adult. Living on your own is expected." I turned back to face the window, tears prickling in the corner of my eyes. *Please don't cry. Not here, not now…*

"My stepdad was a real prick. Did things to me. You know, the sort of things you should never do to a child," Sydney said, softly.

We were both silent for a few minutes.

"I'm sorry that happened to you, but that's not what this is, okay? I didn't do anything with Ian. I thought he was nice…"

But I couldn't help thinking about that look in his eyes when he'd had too much to drink, the roughness of his hands and lips as he practically tried to assault me on his couch. I shuddered at the memory.

"He's the adult, Willow. And you're the child. There's no reason for him to be hanging around you like that, luring you up to his apartment. You did nothing wrong. He's the creep, okay? And I'm glad nothing happened, but if it did … you could tell me, okay?"

She reached over, in a surprising gesture, and took my hand in her hers. She squeezed it softly then let it go.

"Okay," I said, wiping away tears with the back of my hand.

"Here's my number." She tucked a slip of paper into my bag, then looked forward, adjusting her seat and preparing to drive.

"Thank you," I said, staring at the side of her face. "And I'm sorry about your stepdad."

"Me too."

We were silent for the entire ride home, our last ride for at least three months. When she pulled up to drop me off in front of my trailer, she said, "Have a good summer, Willow. And don't forget to call me if you need anything. Anything at all, promise?"

"I promise." As much as I hated to admit it, I was going to miss seeing Sydney this summer.

Chapter Fifteen

GHOSTS

CURRENT DAY

The front garden of the Ashcrofts' lake house had changed from its former glory days. The grass was overgrown and populated by weeds. The house itself, while still magnificent, looked rundown—the formerly pristine paint was peeling; shutters hung loose from their hinges. Over the last two decades, the life had been sucked out of Ian Ashcroft's former home.

Over the years, I'd thought about them—the whole Ashcroft family. Blake and Chloe. Ian and his ex-wife. How quickly life had come unraveled in a matter of seconds.

Choices. They seem so small in the day-to-day spectrum of

things, but they matter. Every choice we make has consequences. I know that better than anyone...

Even though I'd been gone from Hillendale for a long time before moving back, I knew some things about the Ashcroft family. I'd kept up with them a bit over the years. In the days of social media, it was hard not to keep up with people you grew up with. Sometimes, even when you were trying to avoid them, they sprung up in your news feeds or social media suggestions. You couldn't always run from the past, even when you really wanted to.

I stepped up to the front door of the Ashcroft home. I took the heavy brass knocker in my hand and gave three sharp knocks. I wasn't sure if anyone still lived here, but I had to know.

If anyone had a reason to harass me here in Hillendale, it was this family.

Through the grapevine, I'd heard that Mrs. Ashcroft got remarried. She was living abroad with her new husband, hopefully enjoying her new life. But Chloe and Ian...

When the door swung open, I barely recognized her.

Chloe was still beautiful, long and lean; her swan-like neck delicate and exotic. But her face had aged; there were creases in the corners of her mouth, frown lines between her eyes.

"Well, look what the cat dragged in. Willow Roberts!" She was just as crude as I remembered, though.

Chloe reached out and tugged on my wrist, pulling me inside, almost like she had been expecting me.

"I'm sorry, I didn't come to visit. I can only stay for a minute," I said, stopping in the front foyer. I didn't want to be back in this house. Didn't want to see this family.

But I couldn't help looking around—it looked exactly the same, but older. The fancy furniture in the great room, the leatherbound books in rows. And the grand staircase leading upstairs … that awful, gaudy chandelier…

I forced myself to pull away from it all, to focus only on Chloe. She, like the house, was only a flicker of her former glory. Brilliant, but crumbling.

"How have you been, Chloe?"

Chloe smirked. She was wearing a long white dressing gown that looked like something my great-grandmother would have worn. But with her white-blonde hair and translucent eyes, it almost suited her, giving her the impression of being an angel. Or a ghost.

Chloe shifted from foot to foot, restless. "I'm doing just fine. Why are you here, Willow? If you didn't come to visit or see me, then what do you want?" She was the same old Chloe, cutting straight to the chase.

"Well, I'm back in town, temporarily. Just while I fix up my family's old house. I'm going to sell it or rent it out…" Realizing that I was rambling, I stopped and took a deep breath. "Look, Chloe. I've had some trouble since coming back. Someone put a creepy fake corpse in my house that looked like Kathi Jo."

Chloe lifted her eyebrows but didn't respond. I wondered if she already knew. In a town like this one, it only took a few hours for news to spread like wildfire around the lake.

I might as well burst into flames… They all know what happened.

"And someone broke into my house the other day too," I continued.

Chloe leaned her head to the side, narrowing her eyes. "And?"

"And … I don't know. It's been awful," I said, lamely.

"No, that's not what you were going to say… You think it was me or something? Why the hell would I mess with you, Willow?" Chloe said, crossing her arms across her bony chest in defense.

If I closed my eyes and listened to her voice, I could almost imagine we hadn't aged at all. That we were back here, right here … at a party in her house, her treating me like shit as usual…

But she had a point—why did I come here? To accuse her of something? And if so … what was I accusing her of?

"I'm sorry if that's how it sounded, Chloe. Of course,

I'm not accusing you of doing anything to me... I'm just checking in with everyone I know in town. Everyone I knew back then ... to see if you had any idea who would do this to me," I said. I sounded desperate, but that's exactly how I was feeling these days. Desperate to figure it out. Desperate for my life to resume some version of "normal" again...

Chloe dropped her arms and they smacked painfully against her bony sides.

"I don't think about you, Willow. Or about Kathi Jo. That was all a long time ago. It's probably some stupid kids messing with you ... all those pathetic summer kids that think they run the place when they're here. It was probably one of them." She smiled devilishly at me, knowing her "summer kids" comment would cut me like a knife.

Chloe had never accepted me; perhaps none of them really had.

"Okay. Sorry for bothering you." I turned to walk away.

"Wait."

I whipped back around.

"Aren't you going to ask about the rest of us? Do you even care?" Chloe said.

I looked behind her, as though I almost expected someone else to pop into the room beside us. *Ian.*

"How is your family?" I asked, carefully.

"Well, Dad's sick. He had a stroke several years ago. That's why I'm here. I take care of him and the house now. He's upstairs. And Mom ... well, Mom's off with her new fucking family."

"I'm sorry, Chloe," I said.

I'd heard about Ian's stroke years ago—through the social media monster.

Hearing about his stroke didn't feel as gratifying as I thought it would. The older I got, and the farther from childhood I reached, the more I realized he was predatory. He took advantage of my innocence and vulnerability. For many years, I'd felt guilty—as though I had led him on by spending time with him or going up to his apartment. But now I know that he had no right to make a pass at me.

"Don't be sorry, Willow. This is my life now! I write and paint, hang out all day in this big house by myself... It's not so bad, really." Chloe twirled around like a demented dancer, her voice melodic and strange.

Honestly, that sort of life didn't sound so bad. I, too, spent most of my days alone now that I was getting divorced. And I missed writing... I hadn't written anything in years.

But, looking at Chloe, her ghostly transformation, made me think she wasn't well at all. Like Trevor, she had changed. Maybe we all had, and not for the better.

I couldn't get out of there fast enough, especially after

hearing that Ian was still there in the house—sick and suffering from a stroke, but still there…

If Ian Ashcroft is somewhere in this town, then that's not far enough away from me…

SUMMER '00

I sat on the back deck of the lake house, Kathi Jo's borrowed pink jacket wrapped around my shoulders and a cup of tea in my hands. Dad was reading in the Adirondack, another Tom Clancy thriller. Mom was inside in the kitchen, making sticky toffee and banana cream pudding.

This. This is happy, I thought, smiling despite myself.

And I wasn't the only one who seemed happier. All spring I'd been away from home, at work and school … and with Ian for a while. All the while, Mom and Dad seemed to be getting along better than ever. They had seemed excited—exuberant even—to come back to Lake Hillendale this summer.

Part of me couldn't help wondering if maybe my absence was the key to their happiness. Without a kid around to take care of all the time, maybe they had more time to focus on themselves. On their marriage…

I'd only been away from the trailer in Branton for two days, but somehow, being here at the lake … it helped me see things more clearly. Ian was a slimeball and I never wanted to see him again. He had tried to blame the pass on drinking too much, but I didn't believe it. Looking back, perhaps all those fun nights talking and eating pizza ... perhaps, it was always his plan to get me alone and try to take advantage of me.

"I'm headed over to Kathi Jo's. What time should I come home?" I asked my dad. Last summer, I'd run rampant, and they hadn't seemed to mind. Perhaps I was growing up, becoming more mature, because suddenly, I wanted—and needed—them to set more boundaries. Boundaries I had trouble setting for myself.

I also wanted to spend some time with my parents this summer, not just Kathi Jo and the others. Despite everything, I had missed seeing them in the evenings while I was working. I missed family dinners and the sounds of their voices at night.

My dad licked his finger and turned the page. "Not sure. I don't think we have anything going on tonight, honey. So, just go enjoy yourself. Tomorrow though! Don't forget we're going out on the boat."

I gave him a lopsided grin. "Okay, Dad."

It wasn't everything, but it was something. And I was looking forward to going out tomorrow on the speed boat that Dad had rented for the day. He had promised to air up the tubular raft and bring along our fishing poles. *"We'll make an entire day of it,"* he had promised.

I hoped and prayed that whatever had changed

between my parents—whether it was my being gone so often or an improvement in their finances—kept going throughout the summer.

I made my way down the crooked path, tapping the Bigfoot rock for luck on my way, and walked to the water's edge. I approached the bridge. It looked more decrepit than ever, but Kathi Jo said it was sturdy.

I was meeting her and the boys on the other side of the lake today, down at Bart's Bait Shop. They wanted to go fishing in their canoes and try to catch some carp. I had no plans to fish; I just wanted to hang out with my friends. Maybe this year will be different. Less partying at the fire tower and more fun summer activities, I hoped.

As much as I was growing up, I wanted to go back too—to a time when things felt less … complicated and confusing.

❧

The bridge shook under my feet. The lake below was filling up with boats, the way it always did at the beginning of the season. If I closed my eyes, I could almost catch a whiff of sunscreen and bug spray in the air. *Ah, summer.*

Kathi Jo, Trevor, Tommy, and Blake were waiting in the bait shop parking lot in Blake's truck when I arrived.

Seeing their faces was like seeing old ghosts—the kind you welcome and want to return.

Blake was behind the wheel, his red truck shined up good. There was a trailer hooked to the back of it, two bright red canoes strapped down on it.

"Hey, guys!" But as I approached, I could hear the sounds of people arguing.

"Oh, shut the hell up!" Kathi Jo yelled. She was in the passenger seat. Trevor and Tommy were stuffed together in the cab.

"What's going on?" As I walked up to Blake's side, he shot me a warning glare that stopped me in my tracks. For a brief second, I wondered if he knew about me spending time alone with his dad.

But then his face morphed into a tight smile. "Tell Kathi Jo to stop flirting with that asshole in there. He's such an old creep and she's totally into him."

"Bart, the old guy?" I asked, stunned.

Bart had been running the bait shop since I was a little kid. He seemed like a chatty old man, but harmless just the same.

"Yeah, he has the hots for Kathi Jo. Always flirting with her, talking about her tits. Telling her to ditch us and cover up her young, hot body. And instead of telling him where to shove it, she just giggles and teases him. She likes it, I guess."

Blake's eyes were hard as pennies, and for the first

time, I could see his father in him. Was he delusional? Of course Kathi Jo didn't have the hots for old man Bart.

"Relax." Tommy leaned forward in his seat and placed a firm hand on Blake's shoulder. "Let's just go fishing, yeah?" Tommy opened his door and scooted over, giving me room. Trevor gave me a silly, lopsided smile. He looked older and taller, but silly as usual.

"Whatever. Let's just go," Blake said, turning up the volume on his stereo. I leaned in and touched Kathi Jo's arm, but she flinched when I did it.

"You okay?" But she ignored me, staring out of the passenger window, eyes wet with tears.

That day, we fished and swam. We didn't even drink on the water.

Marco Polo. Cannonballs. Exploring the rocky shore of Hillendale, scooping up hidden "treasures"—intricate shells, silky smooth rocks, and cups of imported sand that made us feel almost as if we were somewhere far away from it all—from Hillendale, and from Ian across town. Even Blake and Kathi Jo seemed happy that day, despite their argument from earlier.

That was our last truly good day of summer.

Chapter Sixteen

BRUISES

CURRENT DAY

I made a list of suspects. Who had a reason to target me? To bring back all these things to the surface? Who knew the truth about Kathi Jo? I wondered.

I made a list of people's names, everyone I could think of: the Ashcroft family, Bart, Tommy, Trevor...

I added Isabella and Kathi Jo's biological dad, whose name I didn't know, with a bunch of question marks to the list.

Who else? My thoughts drifted back to old stories of devil worshippers in the woods. In the 1980s, there was this thing called Satanic Panic. All over the U.S., there were reports and stories of satanic ritual abuse. But later, those claims were considered to be unfounded ... no evidence it was real. Some called it mass hysteria.

But could there have been someone or some group back then ... some creep in the woods by the fire tower, watching us? Some stranger who targeted Kathi Jo? Did someone kidnap her all those years ago...?

But then I remembered the note—the one Kathi Jo left her mother: *I can't stay here anymore. Sorry, mom.* I'd never seen the note myself, only heard about it through my own parents. So, I couldn't be a hundred percent certain. *What if Kathi Jo didn't write that letter? What if someone else had left it behind?*

My head ached with the stress of it all. I didn't want to go back to the lake house. I was tired and the sun was setting over Hillendale, but I needed to check for more notes. I couldn't have the crew walking in there in the morning, finding a mysterious note, and calling the police.

This time, before heading to the lake house, I opened the trunk of my car. The Beretta 92 was still in its original hard case. It came that way from the dealer. *I really should take it with me for protection this time*, I thought.

I'd taken the gun out two or three times since making the purchase, but I'd never fired it. The dealer showed me how to load it, take it apart, and clean it. He assured me that guns don't go off unless you pull the trigger, but still ... the thought of having it near me unnerved me. It made me feel afraid. With or without protection, I felt fear.

My husband Jason and I met at a teachers' workshop. He seemed funny and kind. Charismatic. When Jason entered a room, he made it brighter—I don't know how to explain it, but it's true.

On the flip side, when Jason got angry or when he was in a bad mood in general, he also knocked out the lights. I used to think that Jason could lower the temperature in the room with a single breath when he got angry. His moods were unpredictable, like the weather, but what frustrated me most was that he was able to control them in public. My fellow teachers at the school were drawn in by his charm, like gnats in a spider web.

I, too, was once seduced by Jason's charm.

He would smile and laugh in public, but scold me at home—why did I embarrass him? Why did I flirt with that new male teacher? Why didn't I back him up with those unreasonable parents?!

It was a never-ending test and no matter how hard I studied, I couldn't pass it.

The first time Jason put his hands on me, it seemed like a mistake. We were in a heated argument over our finances, that went too far; he reached out and placed his hands on my shoulders. Then he shook me, hard.

The second time was months later, and by then, I'd

nearly forgotten the first time. That time he pulled my hair and gripped my forearm, squeezing so hard he left thumb prints on the soft skin on the underside.

The third time was the last time, and that's when I left. I bought the gun before filing for divorce. I kept it with me when I left town, the locked case beside me wherever I went. But then, when I got here, I thought about how things could go too far, how accidents could happen … what if I shoot someone by accident thinking it was Jason breaking in? What if I accidentally shoot myself?

The gun had been locked up in the car ever since arriving to Hillendale. But now, I toyed with the idea of taking it out. Going back to the lake house after seeing the intruder felt risky.

I should take it with me. I know I should.

But I closed the trunk and locked my car, then I crossed the bridge on foot again. The crew was set to return in the morning, and I needed one last look at the house. If there were more clues or notes … I needed to get them first.

I entered the lake house through the back door this time, slipping silently through the dark living room and kitchen. I stopped in the dining area, unmoving, listening in the dark.

I couldn't hear a thing, yet somehow, I could sense something in the dark.

Suddenly, my decision to leave the gun in my trunk felt stupid and naive. *Like the sort of mistake I might live to regret...*

When I stepped into the main sitting room, I reached for the switch. But just as the lights were about to pop on, I heard something brush by behind me. Before I could turn, someone reached around, gripping my neck in the dark.

"Get the fuck out of Hillendale," the attacker whispered in my ear, in a voice that sounded vaguely familiar. I grabbed at their forearms, clawing desperately as their grip tightened around my throat. My breath shortened as they applied pressure on my windpipe ... *tighter, tighter, tighter...*

I lifted one foot then another, desperately kicking backwards in the dark.

"Please ... don't," I rasped, consciousness slipping away.

SUMMER '00

For a while, things were better. Easier. Less complicated. As though a weight had been lifted—*I can breathe again now that I'm in Hillendale.*

But, like all things attached to the dog days of summer, it had to come to an end.

Parties at the fire tower resumed. Stories of devil

worshippers and dark nighttime things returned. We drank too much, laughed too hard, woke up in the mornings, feeling like death, only to do it all over again.

But it wasn't that simple. Not anymore. Something had shifted in Hillendale: Mom and Dad were fighting again, low irritated voices rising to full-volume shouting now. Dad was back at it again, blowing our money away at the casino, leaving Mom to deal with the mess.

The casino made me think of Ian. He was one of the head guys in Greenville—*could he ban my dad from getting in if I asked him to? Would that even stop their marriage from unraveling? Would it be worth reaching out to him about it?*

The thought of talking to Ian again filled me with dread, though.

The gambling was a thread, a tiny piece in the loosely woven fabric of my parents' marriage. The more Dad tugged, the more it all came apart, as though it had never been one whole unit in the first place.

We were all coming unraveled ... bit by bit—my friendship with Kathi Jo turning looser, becoming less defined. And I couldn't stop thinking about Ian, how his hands had turned rough in an instant, how the pressure to do more, be more, give more had felt so intense. I hoped to never see him again.

As though thinking about Ian triggered him to think of me too, he called the lake house in early July, right after the Fourth and the annual firework celebration on the water. It had been fun, but as usual, Kathi Jo and the others wanted to break away on their own to get drunk and high.

"It's your boss on the phone. He says it's important. Wants to discuss the upcoming work schedule for fall," my mother said. She handed me the cordless phone and turned back to her coffee. She'd given up on cooking at the lake house. Most days, we ate sandwiches, cereal, or nothing at all, it seemed.

He? Candy could be a gruff woman, but certainly not mistaken for a man.

I took the phone and slipped out on the front porch. Taking a seat in the rocker, I tugged on the antennae to combat the static. "Hello? Candy?"

"Willow, it's me. Oh, I can't tell you how much I've missed your voice and your company." My chest tightened at the rich swirl of Ian's voice; a mixture of sadness and fear ran through me. *What was he thinking, calling me here at my parents' house after what he tried to do?!*

As though he could hear my thoughts through the phone, he said, "I told your mom I was your boss from the sweet shop. I hope that's okay. I didn't want them to think anything weird about me calling you. Because I just worry about you, you know? You're like a second daughter to me..."

My thoughts darkened. If Mom and Dad knew more

about my life, or Ian for that matter, then they'd all know Candy, my boss, was a woman.

The screen door popped open, and Dad lumbered out, looking sad and pathetic after a late night spent gambling and arguing with Mom. I'd heard the sound of glass breaking earlier, muffled by the fireworks, and I'd wished more than anything that I was living at Kathi Jo's house instead of here.

My dad looked at me, as though noticing me for the first time, and gave a little smile. I clutched the phone so hard my knuckles turned white.

"Thanks for calling, Candy, but I have to go. I won't be returning to work, but I wish you the best," I said, woodenly. Then I clicked the off button and carried the phone inside, letting the screen door slam shut behind me.

～

Mom and Dad weren't the only ones fighting. I'd heard the bickering and seen the nasty looks passing between Kathi Jo and Blake all summer. Whatever had blossomed between them last summer was slowly withering away.

That night, three weeks before the end of my summer vacation, Kathi Jo told me a secret.

We had been drinking Seagrams, the peach kind that tasted like marmalade and bitters. It was half past midnight, and I couldn't help feeling a sense of ease, a comforting sense of pleasure at having my friend all to myself, if only for one night.

Her mom was downstairs sleeping, her soft snores like kittens purring, rising through the air vents on the floor of Kathi Jo's bedroom. Isabella's snores were a welcoming sound, much better than my parents' arguing.

But then Kathi Jo pushed up her sleeves and showed me her bruises. There was one, two, three, four of them, a couple looked purple and new, the others greenish yellow from something that had happened a week or two earlier.

"Please don't tell me he did that to you." I grabbed her arm and pulled it toward me, resting it hand up in my lap. I stroked the tender flesh then looked into her eyes. We were sitting cross-legged on the bed facing each other, knees nearly touching, the way we did years ago when we were kids. Before things like boys and hormones went and fucked up everything.

"I can't tell you that," Kathi Jo said.

"But I don't understand." But of course I understood. Blake was a fucking asshole.

"I love him, you know? But he gets so pissed. And he has no reason to be. I've never cheated. I barely look at the other guys or talk to anyone else at school. But when Blake gets drunks, he gets so mad. And sometimes he hurts me by accident," Kathi Jo said.

"These bruises don't look accidental to me," I said, carefully touching one of the green bruises with my thumb.

"It's not completely his fault. His dad was rough and controlling with his mom. Hard on him and his brothers and Chloe, too. He told me all of this; he cried and begged me to forgive him. Said he doesn't want to end up like his father."

Kathi Jo's words felt like shrapnel in my chest, heavy with nowhere to go. *Could this be true? Was Ian violent with his family?*

"You have to end it with Blake. I'm sorry, Kat, but if he did it once then he'll do it again. Whatever happened to him growing up with his dad was shitty, but that's no excuse for hurting you. And you don't have to put up with it just because some bad things happened to him when he was a kid."

Kathi Jo nodded, chewing on the edge of her thumb. "I think I'll break up with him tomorrow. It's the right thing to do."

"Good! And I'll go with you if you're too scared to do it," I offered.

Kathi Jo was still nodding and gnawing. Her eyes were faraway, in a place where I couldn't reach her anymore. I missed that confident, happy harpy in the lake. The one who laughed and made up stories. The one whose boyfriend didn't cause her bruises.

And me … I've changed too. We all have. God, how much we've changed…

She was my best friend in the whole world, and I was hers. But I wasn't sure how to help her.

"Willow?" Kathi Jo was still chewing on her bottom lip.

"What is it?" I asked.

"Just promise me. Promise me you won't tell anyone about the bruises. About what he did to me…"

I nodded. "Of course not. You're my best friend. I promise I won't tell."

Chapter Seventeen

THE FALLEN

CURRENT DAY

There's a loud banging sound, growing louder in my brain.

Is this what dying sounds like?

There was someone in the lake house, their hands around my throat.

I can't breathe … I'm going to die here…

But then: *Bang, bang, bang!*

Followed by a beautiful rush of oxygen to my brain. My attacker's grip had loosened from around my throat.

Someone is banging on the back door!

"I'm coming in!" A man's voice shouted as my knees hit the floor. Gasping for air; my breath like shards of glass in my throat.

Suddenly, my attacker pushed. *Falling, falling, falling* … my face smacked the solid wood floor, my newly found breath knocked right out of my chest again.

I heard shouting and the scuffle of heavy boots, then the sound of the front door slamming.

"Are you okay? He ran."

I peeled my face off the floor, choking for air, and then I felt the pull of strong arms around me. Someone lifting me back on my feet.

But then, I was whisked right off them again; my savior was carrying me over to the sofa.

"Trevor?"

He sat me down on the sofa and paced back and forth in front of me, running his hands through his hair. He was wearing heavy boots and dark blue jeans. He had his cell phone out in his hand, getting ready to call for help, I presumed.

"Trevor, is that you?" I repeated, hands rubbing at the red, raw skin around my neck. My face hurt too, like I'd been smacked with a metal frying pan.

"Yes. I can't see where they went but I'm calling the cops right now, don't worry…" Trevor said.

"Wait. Don't do that yet, please," I croaked. My head was muddled, and my throat was on fire, but I knew I didn't need the cops.

Trevor looked at me, phone frozen in his hand. A sliver of moonlight cast through the blinds, striking his face. He looked so rough, like he'd been through hell and back.

"What are you doing here, Trevor?" I asked, my voice hoarse and painful.

Trevor scratched his beard and stepped closer. "I was watching you. I heard about the incident with the mannequin that looked like Kathi Jo. I wanted to know what you were up to."

"Me? Why?" I kept rubbing my neck, still grateful I could breathe again, as though any moment now, the breath might be stolen from me again...

"I know it was you who took my car that night ... all those years ago. I came out of the party, and it was gone. I saw you come back and drop it off later that night, but I never said anything," Trevor said, shakily. He looked so serious, stone cold and jaded. Not the smiling, teasing boy of my youth.

"So what?" I croaked. "I went looking for Blake and Kathi Jo that night. I didn't find them, so I brought it back. Wait. Are you the one who left me that stupid note?"

"Note? No, I didn't leave a note, Willow. I was watching you. Just checking things out ... and then I saw you crossing the bridge to the other side in the pitch darkness," he said, still pacing and wringing his hands. Tommy had mentioned some drug problems; I wondered, for a moment, if he might be using again.

"You followed me all the way here from my apartment?" I said. *Could Trevor be the real danger here? I couldn't help wondering.*

"Not exactly. I mean, yes. I did. I hung back a bit and then I crossed over. But when I came up, I could hear a struggle going on. I looked in and saw you. Saw hands around your neck…" Trevor grimaced.

"Did you see their face, my attacker's?" I asked, hopefully.

Trevor shook his head, but I wasn't sure if I believed him. The thought of him following me, hanging around the lake house and my apartment, well, it gave me the creeps.

"I didn't do anything that night when I took your car. I told the truth about that night, except the part where I went looking for Blake and Kathi Jo before … before it happened. I promise, I'm telling the truth," I told him.

But it wasn't the full truth … not really.

SUMMER '00

"Party at Blake's tonight! Come meet me at seven. Trevor's going to drive us in his new Volvo," Kathi Jo gushed into the phone.

"What?" This couldn't be real, could it? Less than twenty-four hours ago, she had confessed to me that

Blake was violent, that she planned to break up with him.

"Look, I know what I said last night. But, regardless, Chloe and the others are still my friends. And don't worry, Blake apologized. It's all just one big misunderstanding, okay? Let's do this for us, Willow! A party ... one last time before summer ends, okay? We only have a few weeks left," Kathi Jo whined.

I knew I should say no. For her best interests, and mine. I didn't want to go to a party at the Ashcrofts'. I hated that stupid, big house, and if it were going to be a night for celebrating "us" and "friendship", I would have preferred another night alone with my best friend. Plus, being there would remind me of Ian, his fake kindness and his too-rough hands...

But these people are her friends. Unlike you, she's stuck here all year long, I tried to remind myself.

"If you really want to go, then I guess I'll go with you. But I don't really want to," I spoke.

"Love you, Willow! Thank you. You're the best. See you in about an hour," Kathi Jo gushed, then hung up the phone.

I didn't bother with make-up or neat clothes. I tugged on a long-sleeved shirt, jacket, and jeans—it was uncharacteristically cool that evening—and I tucked my hair into a small baseball cap I'd borrowed from Sydney one night. I missed my work friends and I missed Sydney, even if she was bitchy most of the time.

I didn't miss Ian, not anymore…

Part of me wished I could take Kathi Jo home with me, take her home to Branton. Nothing else from this town appealed to me anymore, only her…

On the way to the party, Kathi Jo rode up front with Trevor. He was loud and obnoxious the whole way, telling jokes and playing music too loud. Unfortunately, I was stuck in the back, stretching my legs across the seat.

Moments later, we picked up Tommy, then drove up the hill to the Ashcroft house.

"It's good to see you," Tommy said, squishing in beside me as I tucked in my legs. He was always so nice. Nicer than the others. I studied his side profile, the thickening sideburns and his chiseled jaw. He looked more handsome than I remembered.

The Ashcroft mansion looked like a ghoulish monster as we pulled up to it, the lake like a thick, black cloak floating around behind it.

Deep down, I knew there was no way Ian would come here. He was across town, at his apartment, probably watching some boring old war movie or something, drinking his old man cocktails. But just being in his family home gave me the creeps.

I felt a flash of déjà vu as I followed Tommy, Trevor, and Kathi Jo to the pool at the back. Chloe and Blake were already in the hot tub; Blake was holding a beer and Chloe was drinking something red and spicy-looking from a long-stemmed wine glass.

"Hello, my loves!" Chloe gleamed, looking at everyone but me. When her eyes finally rested on mine, she puckered up her lips as though just looking at me gave her heartburn.

"Hopefully there's enough room for everyone. This hot tub only fits six and not all of us are skinny!" She poked at Tommy's thickening waistline in his swim trunks, but again, her eyes drifted over to me and then down to my stomach.

Fuck her.

I'd gained nearly fifteen pounds since last summer, but I was beyond caring these days.

If being skinny meant acting these assholes, then I didn't want it anymore.

I stripped out of my jacket and jeans and turned away from the hot tub.

"There are wine coolers or the hard stuff. What do you want, Willow?" Kathi Jo asked. She was bent over the cooler, digging her fingers through ice. Oblivious to Chloe's meanness.

"Nothing. I'm not drinking tonight." The others cooed and teased, but I didn't care about that either. I hated drinking, and watching them when they were drunk made me realize how dumb they all looked too.

I adjusted the straps of my one-piece bathing suit, then dove headfirst into the pool.

"Watch out for the tsunami!" I heard Chloe teasing behind me.

~

The party was over before it'd even started. They were all loud and drunk, and I couldn't get Kathi Jo away from Blake's side. Now that I knew about the bruises, I noticed everything about him—his possessiveness, his mean streak, the way Kathi Jo changed completely around him.

Although Blake didn't seem angry at her tonight, he still seemed clingy and annoying. He kept pulling her in closer to him, wrapping his arm around her neck so tight it looked like she was uncomfortable. I couldn't stop staring at her faded bruises and it pissed me off that no one else seemed to notice, or care.

Finally, I excused myself from the natatorium, but no one noticed that either. I sauntered through the empty hallways of the Ashcroft manor, fingers sweeping over the walls. The expensive artwork and the family photos. Ian looked happy with his wife and his children. Not like the kind of man you'd expect to make a pass at an underaged girl.

In the kitchen, I found a 2l bottle of Diet Coke and

carried the whole thing to the sitting room I'd seen in the back. There were rows and rows of DVDs. Many I hadn't seen before, but I picked up an old favorite—*Titanic*.

I'll watch it myself and drink my soda, then perhaps take a nap, I decided.

The walls of the sitting room were adorned with more pictures, mostly Blake and Chloe as children and pre-teens. They looked so much alike when they were younger, with their light eyes and hair, that they could have been twins.

On one wall, there was a bulletin board with a dry erase marker. Someone had written Kathi Jo and Chloe's names. *BFFs 4 Life* it said beside it. Each "I" dotted with a stupid, tiny heart. I could only assume Chloe had written it.

Apparently, Chloe and Kathi Jo had grown closer than I'd realized during the school year while I was far away in Branton…

~

The next time I opened my eyes, the boat was sinking.

I sat up on the couch, stomach gurgling from all that soda and no food, and looked at the fancy grandfather clock on the wall. It was half past midnight.

I wanted more than anything to go home, but with everyone drinking, I knew there was a good chance—

and it was probably smart—that we would all stay here for the night.

Sleepily, I ambled back out to the pool and deck area, but only Tommy, Trevor, and Chloe were outside. They were smoking now, thick cigars that probably belonged to Ian.

"Do you want one?" Trevor offered, blowing a ring of smoke toward my face. He looked like a little kid playing dress-up, pretending to be the Godfather or something.

"No. Where's Kathi Jo?" I asked, hoping she hadn't snuck off to a room to have sex with Blake. *Gross.*

"They left," Chloe shrugged.

"Left? But they were drinking."

Chloe snorted then coughed as she inhaled, leaning forward in her seat.

"Quite the Little Miss Goody Two-shoes, aren't you?" she giggled.

"Not really," I mumbled, looking at the boys. They looked stoned, like maybe they were smoking more than just cigars.

Tommy seemed to be the only one listening.

"I'm sure they're fine, Willow," Tommy said, stubbing out his cigar in a fancy, chiseled ash tray next to the hot tub.

"Were they fighting when they left?" I asked him.

Tommy shook his head, but Trevor piped in, "Yeah. Blake *was* pissed off about something. I guess they took a drive so they could talk. Leave them be, Willow. Just a lovers' quarrel."

In a house this big, why would they need to leave the party just to have a private chat? It sounded to me like Blake wanted to sneak her away, possibly so he could hurt her again...

"I'm going inside to lie down," I told them, unsure if anyone was listening to me anyway.

Butterflies of panic invaded my chest as I went back inside the house. What if Kathi Jo was drunk and decided to break up with Blake on her own? What if he hurt her, crashed the car, or did any number of stupid things?

As I paced back and forth in the kitchen, I couldn't shake off the images of those bruises. The way Kathi Jo's whole demeanor changed when Blake was upset.

Trevor's keys were still on the kitchen counter. I scooped them up and slipped out the front door quietly. I knew how to drive. Sydney had let me drive her truck around the laundromat parking lot a few times. It was a stick shift and if I could drive that, then I could manage Trevor's little prissy Volvo.

I started the engine, praying Trevor didn't come running out to stop me. I didn't have my license yet, but at least I was sober. If they weren't going to help Kathi Jo, then I would.

~

It wasn't hard to find them. Blake's truck was parked near the shelter house and neither of them were inside it. Parking the Volvo behind his truck, I got out and moved as quickly as I could through the thick, black trees.

I swatted at branches and brush, the whole forest shifting into something monstrous and dangerous in the dark. The tree limbs reaching out like sharpened claws, the brush like hidden devil people waiting to get me…

I heard them before I saw them. Blake and Kathi Jo were shouting, their voices echoing through the chilly night sky.

But mostly, it was Blake I heard. His voice boomed loudly overhead. And Kathi Jo was crying, her whimpers animalistic in the dark.

"I wasn't flirting with Trevor! I wouldn't do that to you. Look, I don't think it's meant to be, okay? We should take a break, just for a little while…" I heard Kathi Jo crying.

"You fucking bitch." I heard the venom in his words, and I took off running.

The stairs to the tower were endless, my shoes slapping each metal stair, reverberating all the way to the top of the tower. Each step groaned with my weight, but I knew they were at the top.

"Leave her alone!" I shouted over and over with each

step I took. Finally, when I burst through the top, Blake had Kathi Jo by the neck with both hands. He was squeezing, her eyes large and afraid, bulging from her face...

"Stop! You'll kill her, you psycho!" I screamed, running towards him.

"Oh, she's fine," Blake said, suddenly releasing his grip. He stepped back from Kathi Jo, and she let out a gasp, clutching her neck. She was bent over, catching her breath as I stepped up to Blake. *That bastard!*

"I'm fine, Willow. Just go on home, okay?" Kathi Jo's voice rasped from behind me.

"No, I won't go home. I'm going to call the cops and have him arrested," I said.

"Is that so, bitch?" Blake sneered. He closed the gap between us, stalking towards me, fists clenched at his sides.

He lifted his arm as though he might throw a punch at me, so I quickly stepped to the side. He turned back around, sneering.

"You're not going to do a damn thing about it, Willow!" Blake yelled.

"Wanna bet?" I stepped closer to him. So close I could smell his awful summer smells. He wasn't honeysuckle and heartache; he was hemlock and horror.

That's when I shoved him, hard as I could. It happened so quickly, but it was also slow ... like the reel of a horror movie, garbled and strange. Blake stumbled back, the back of his kneecaps connecting with the safety bar. It was too low, never a safety bar at all. We used to joke about that all the time…

Blake's eyes widened as he stumbled, losing his balance … arms pinwheeling in the air…

I watched in horror as he tumbled back, falling *down, down, down* … like a devil floating through the night sky.

Chapter Eighteen

FROM A DIFFERENT ANGLE

CURRENT DAY

When I thought back to that final summer—how it all came undone, untethered in a single moment—the details became sort of fuzzy. I never told anyone about what happened that night at the fire tower. Not my husband or my parents ... not my friends or colleagues. Not even the therapist I saw for two years in my twenties.

The only other person who knew what I did was there when it happened ... and now she was gone. A runaway. Missing. *Possibly dead or murdered.*

It's strange—guilt consumed me for many years, but it wasn't guilt for taking Blake's life. I shed no tears over Blake Ashcroft. He was abusing my friend and I tried to protect her. But I felt guilty for letting it happen, for not doing something sooner. For not noticing, for being too caught up in my own twisted concerns over Blake's father ... and for agreeing to go to the party that night, and not keeping a good enough eye on Kathi Jo.

Because of me, she left town. She ran away and never looked back. That's the best-case scenario. The worst ... I don't even want to think about that. I don't want to imagine what may have happened.

Did she take her own life? Did she run away somewhere and run into trouble, into someone much worse than Blake out there in the world?

Was she unable to forgive me for what I'd done, unable to face Hillendale ever again?

The note—the one she left her mother, saying goodbye—why didn't she leave me one? How could she leave me there to pick up the pieces?

I didn't know all the answers, but I did know one thing: *someone has been fucking with me. Someone who knows about what I did to Blake.*

I climbed the steps of the tower. They groaned under my weight as I forced myself to *climb, climb, climb...*

I hadn't climbed these steps since that night, since the night I took Blake's life.

But I had to face it now. *No looking back. No looking down.*

When I reached the top, I was gasping for breath and

sweating in my thick cream sweatshirt. I peeled it off, exposing my thin, flimsy tank top underneath.

I walked to the edge, step by step, and leaned against the rail. From up here, I could see the entire town of Hillendale. The lake and the forest, all the tiny houses ... even the large house on the lake that belonged to Ian Ashcroft. Up here, I could see who was coming or going. The perfect lookout.

I didn't want to look down, afraid I would see him ... his lifeless limbs bent at odd angles on the ground. But instead, I saw nothing—the trees shifting in the breeze. The ghosts of who we once were that summer.

All of it ruined, because of me. And a secret I'd buried so deep that I'd nearly forgotten what I'd done to Blake. For so long, I had tried to pretend that he died as a result of an accidental drunken fall, just like they all assumed.

I stepped back from the edge and slid down on the metal floor of the rooftop. I had a sudden urge to howl and scream, to make my pain echo all through Hillendale.

There were words written everywhere on the rooftop walls of the tower. Some graffiti, but mostly scratchy words.

Gina Franklin is a whore.
Jimbo was here.
Matt + Beatrice = 4 Life

Karina is a slut

Some of the writing looked recent, teens in Hillendale still sneaking up here, wreaking havoc in the dead of night. But some of the writing seemed older, more faded.

R.I.P. Blake

And a few other sentiments that memorialized his death.

But one line stood out to me, above all else. Tiny letters, written with such force and anger, that they were less drawn, and more engraved, someone digging in the rusted paint.

Blake didn't fall KJR got what she deserved.

And the dot of the "i" in "didn't", marked with a tiny heart.

SUMMER '00

The best way to hide a body is not to hide it at all.

That's why I left him there, smashed on the ground at the bottom of the tower, displayed in plain sight.

When it happened, there was a sharp cracking sound at the bottom. Or maybe I just imagined that.

I charged down the metal stairs, the whole tower shaking under my weight, or so it felt. I don't know what I thought I would find. Obviously, he couldn't be saved. Nobody falls that far and lives to talk about it.

His neck was bent at an odd angle, as were his arms and legs. I tried to move his head, to see if he was alive … but his neck made this creaking sound, like the hinges on a rusty old barn door. That's when I noticed the gooey substance, spreading out from his head and backside, leaking towards my feet on the forest floor.

A sharp scream pierced the air and I turned. Kathi Jo collapsed on the ground beside me. I'd nearly forgotten she was there and hadn't even heard her running down the tower stairs behind me.

Kathi Jo was on the ground at my feet, gripping my calf with both hands, clawing my skin like a feral cat.

"What did you do? What did you do?. What did you do, Willow?" The words running together like one big, jumbled mess. *A mess of bones and brain matter and bodily fluid on the ground. This is a mess we can't clean up…*

We have to go. We have to go right now, I thought, suddenly.

"Get up." I tugged on Kathi Jo's arm. When that wasn't enough, I turned and lifted her onto both of her feet and turned her away from the body. For a moment, the entire forest was spinning, and it felt like I was outside my own body, watching someone else march their best friend away from the scene of a crime. The scene of a crime I'd committed.

This can't be real, this can't be real, this can't be real…

"We have to go," I choked out the words, again.

For the first time, Kathi Jo looked at me. She looked like she'd never seen me before in her life. Hell, I probably wouldn't recognize myself after this either.

She glanced back over her shoulder at the heaping mass that used to be Blake, her face crumpling and legs wobbling, threatening to topple off-balance all over again.

"Come on. We have to walk. We're leaving. Let the police think he jumped or accidentally fell. He was drunk… You broke up with him and he dropped you off on the side of the road, so you left him and walked home. What happened to him after, you don't know anything about that."

Kathi Jo was mumbling incoherently as I led her through the thick pine, past the gnarly trunks of the forest. The forest seemed like a foreign jungle all of a sudden, everything different and unrecognizable.

"Repeat it back to me. Do it now," I said, as we reached Trevor's Volvo parked at the edge of the forest. Less than fifteen minutes ago, I'd sat behind the wheel of this car.

Fifteen minutes ago, I wasn't a murderer. But now I am…

Kathi Jo stared at the back of Blake's truck. I knew

what she was thinking—he would never drive it again. Never breathe again. Because of me, Blake was dead.

I barely remembered driving Kathi Jo home that night. All I remembered was tucking her pink jacket I had borrowed around her like a blanket and asking her to repeat the plan back to me. *Repeat, repeat, repeat …* and all I could think about was Blake's face, that vacant expression, eyes confused as his body connected with open air. How scared he looked when he was *falling, falling, falling…*

Kathi Jo's teeth were chattering despite the jacket. She had tucked her knees into a ball against her chest, like a roly poly.

She chattered, face hidden behind her hair, "I broke up with Blake. He dropped me off on Phoenix Lane and I walked the last mile home alone. I figured he'd go back to the party to drink some more… I don't know what happened next."

"Good." I parked at the top of 1 Daisy Lane and reached over to hug her. She flinched at my touch.

"I'm leaving you here. I'm going to take Trevor's Volvo back and leave it at the party. They probably don't even know I was gone. Then I'll make my way back home. Tomorrow, I'll come over in the morning, okay?"

But nothing was okay. Maybe, things would never be okay again.

Ian's son was dead. Kathi Jo's boyfriend was dead.

I was just trying to defend her... I thought he might kill her, throw her off the tower...

I did the right thing, didn't I?

"Will you be okay until we meet up in the morning? Try to get some sleep, yeah?" But the words were stupid and meaningless. Neither Kathi Jo nor I would be sleeping tonight. Hell, I might never sleep again. Every time I closed my eyes, I'd see Blake's face ... the way it looked before the fall and after, broke like a melon on the ground.

"Repeat it back to me. One more time, just to be sure. We have to be careful, Kat. Please."

She repeated it back again. Her teeth had finally stopped chattering.

Before I could tell her goodbye, she jumped out. I stared at her back as she walked towards her house, hunched inside her big pink jacket. I watched her until the darkness swallowed her whole.

I walked all night after dropping off the Volvo, taking a short cut around the lake to make it back home in time before sunrise. I thought I'd die of exhaustion or pass out the moment I crawled into my loft bed, but my brain just wouldn't shut down.

I could barely remember the walk home. I could barely remember a moment of my life before...

I peeled off my shoes and socks. There were blisters on every toe.

I tugged off my shirt and jeans, slipping beneath the sheets in my underwear.

I tried to imagine how the town would react when they discovered Blake's body at the foot of the tower. Faces swirled before my eyes—my parents, Blake's mom, Ian, Chloe. Tommy and Trevor. They would all be so devastated.

I could tell the truth. I was only defending my best friend.

But was there really any proof of that? Kathi Jo would back me up—or would she?

Please let Kathi Jo come over to see me tonight. Or tomorrow, at least. I need to know that she's okay, that she understands why I did it and forgives me…

But Kathi Jo didn't come see me that day, or any day thereafter. The day after I pushed Blake from the tower, Kathi Jo ran away from Hillendale. All she left behind was a simple note, addressed solely to her mother:

I can't stay here anymore. Sorry, Mom.

Chapter Nineteen

WHO'S TO BLAME?

CURRENT DAY

I banged the side of my fists on the Ashcroft door. Only a couple days had passed since I'd last come here, but that felt like a distant memory now.

"OPEN THE HELL UP!" I screamed, pressing my mouth to the thick red door. "I KNOW YOU'RE IN THERE!"

When no one came, I took the knob in my hand. I was surprised when it turned easily. Unlocked.

My attacker was waiting.

I lifted the gun and pointed it at Chloe's smiling face.

"Nice to see you again, Willow." She was sitting cross-legged on a chaise longue, a book folded in her hands.

I stomped into the room; gun still pointed at her stupid face. "You blamed her for what happened to your brother. Did you kill her, Chloe? Is that why you've been fucking with me since I got back to town? You want me to know that you were the one who made her disappear?"

I didn't want to use the gun, but I would if I had to. My heart hammered in my chest like it was filling with bullets.

Chloe cocked her head to one side, studying me in that haughty way she did when we were kids. For the first time, I noticed her bare legs—in a pair of silky shorts, two nasty abrasions were exposed on her shins. *I got her good when I kicked her then. Good! That bitch tried to choke me!*

"Where is Kathi Jo? You didn't attack me for no reason. I know you did something... You know where she is... You know something. What the fuck is it?" I demanded.

Chloe got to her feet, stretching like a cat as though she couldn't be bothered with me. I stepped backed from her as she strode towards me, keeping the gun aimed steadily at her mid-section.

She stopped inches from my face, unfazed by the gun. "Why would I tell you anything?" she said, a slow smile spreading on her ghastly face.

"Because there are things you need to know too,

Chloe. You're right. Blake didn't fall. He and Kathi Jo were up there fighting. But it wasn't her who pushed him, it was me. And given the chance I'd do it again."

Chloe sucked in a sharp breath through her teeth and turned her back on me.

"I never thought Kathi Jo killed my brother. Why would you?"

I ignored her question and skipped straight to my own. "I don't understand. If you didn't know I pushed him and you didn't think it was her either, then why do you blame her, Chloe? What the hell did you do to my friend?" I shouted, the gun shaking wildly in my hand. The safety was still on, and I wasn't sure if I remembered how to flick it off.

"She was having an affair with my father. I found out about it, and I told Blake too. He didn't want to believe me, but it was true. I know it was—"

"Ian? No way." My thoughts wandered shakily back to those late-nights with Ian. Had he also been spending time with Kathi Jo? No. No way. She would have told me…

"I went there one night to surprise him. It was his birthday week, and I thought he'd be excited to see his little girl. But then I heard them … talking and laughing. I saw her stupid pink coat on the floor."

I gasped, the gun sliding from my palm and smacking the marble floor at my feet.

"It wasn't her, Chloe. I had the coat. I had it all fall and winter; she let me borrow it."

Chloe's eyes narrowed and her lips curled.

"So, it was you all along. Stupid, fat, pathetic, forgettable Willow. I guess I wasn't right about everything." Chloe shrugged. "Oh well," she added, with a shaky, forced smile.

"I didn't have an affair with him, Chloe. He tried, but I didn't want to. And Kathi Jo didn't either. Did you hurt her, Chloe? Tell me where she is, please…" I begged.

Chloe leaned her head to one side, eyes studying me. "Oh, Willow, you *must* know that I hurt her. Why else would you set up the dummy in your lake house and cause all this drama to stir up the town again about Kathi Jo?"

"I didn't…" I shook my head back and forth, feeling more confused than ever. "If you didn't leave the mannequin, then who did? I don't understand…"

Again, Chloe shrugged. "Who knows and who cares. As usual, you're boring me to death. Come on, now. I'll show you where Kathi Jo is."

SUMMER '00

They shared her picture on the nightly local news. They even assembled a small army of search parties spreading out like a fan in the town of Hillendale.

But no one found her, and mostly, no one cared. Everyone was too focused on the tragic death of Hillendale's golden boy, Blake Ashcroft.

Blake's family channeled their devastation into fury— they threatened to sue the town, and then the entire county. They blamed everyone and everything for his death—except themselves, of course.

They blamed the tower: it wasn't safe and needed to be torn down, they argued. They blamed the park ranger who made his rounds at night, for not stopping local teens from going up in the tower.

But all of the parents knew what the teens in Hillendale were up to, including the Ashcrofts. They, themselves, had spent time in that very same tower in their youth. It was a lakeside tradition.

They blamed the bait shop for underage liquor sales, although we all knew Blake had no issues with getting alcohol straight from his own parents' liquor cabinet. And, in the end, the Ashcrofts turned on each other—Ian blamed Blake's mother and she blamed him back. Someone should have been there that night to stop him from leaving the house while he was drunk... He was upset about a fight with his girlfriend and about his parents' divorce; either he fell by accident because he was drunk or made a stupid decision and jumped.

I thought my parents would force me to attend Blake's funeral, but they didn't think it was appropriate.

Only close friends and family, they said, as though they didn't even realize I'd spent the past two summers hanging out with Blake and his friends.

Regardless, I was relieved. When we left that summer, we never came back. My parents paid a regular cleaner and rented the place out from time to time, but those summer days of Hillendale died with Blake, and left my life for good just as my best friend had.

Chapter Twenty

HER STORY

SUMMER '00

Kathi Jo's backpack fit snugly across her shoulders, the weight of her extra clothes and sneakers cutting ridges in the soft skin between her shoulders and neck. She couldn't stay in Hillendale. Not after what happened at the tower. Willow might have pushed him, but Blake's death was her fault. She never should have let it get that far. Blake's temper flared when he was drunk and flirting with Trevor was a bad idea. She wanted to end it—if Blake wouldn't let her break up with him then maybe she could force it by making him want to dump her instead. But her plan to flirt with Trevor and piss Blake off backfired, didn't it? Now he was dead, and it was all her fault.

Blake was dead, images of his crooked limbs and stone white face, and his eyes ... once so alive and angry, now flat and dead like marbles. Kathi Jo didn't have a clear-cut plan — all she knew was that she had to go. She would never be able to walk the hallways of Hillendale school without seeing his face, and the tower and the lake... *No, I can't do it. I have to get out of this godforsaken town.*

Even Kathi Jo's best friend was tainted. Could she ever look at Willow again without seeing that thrust of anger, that flash of hate in her eyes when she pushed Blake off the tower?

A plan was forming in her brain though: Kathi Jo had distant family in Montana, her aunt, Ariana, and baby cousin, Cinderella.

Coming here is a mistake, Kathi Jo thought, as she stepped up to the Ashcrofts' front door. The whole house intimidated her—*at least I'll never have to come here again after tonight*, she thought. But she owed Chloe an explanation. She owed her a goodbye.

While Kathi Jo and Willow had become close over the summers, she and Chloe had gotten close during the winter and fall.

Kathi Jo had no plans of telling Chloe the truth ... not the *truth* truth. She wouldn't let anything happen to Willow. Willow had just been trying to defend her when she pushed him...

But Kathi Jo would at least tell Chloe about the fall. She would tell her she was sorry for contributing to his accidental death. That she was so sorry for her loss. That she was leaving and would miss her forever.

"Kat! Speak of the devil..." When the door creaked open, Chloe looked the same as she had the night before —heavy make-up still caked on her face and her bone-white hair combed back straight and perfect like the blade of a knife down her back.

"I-I..." Kathi Jo wasn't sure where to start.

"Come in! I need a drink! Drink with me." Chloe waved a hand and disappeared through the kitchen. Kathi Jo followed, hit with a horrible realization—that maybe Chloe had already heard the news.

In the kitchen, Chloe poured Hpnotiq into a shaker with what looked like gin and ice.

"My mom and dad are gone. They're at the police station, talking to them about my brother's death," Chloe said, her voice casual.

So, she does know then, Kathi Jo realized, in horror. Would the cops be looking for her soon? Did they know about what Willow had done?

"I'm so sorry, Chloe. I loved him so much. I wish..."

"You wish what?" Chloe slammed the drink down on the counter and started pouring another.

"I don't know. I don't know what I wish..." Suddenly, Kathi Jo couldn't think of one good reason for her to be here. She should have kept going, all the way to the bus stop in Greenville. Never should have come to this place —this sad old house on the lake. The place where she lost her virginity to Blake; the place where he hit her for the first time and pinched her arm so hard it bruised.

"Let me show you something." Chloe's eyes were lit with a manic fire; desire or drunkenness, Kathi Jo wasn't sure. She wondered if Chloe were in shock, unable to fully comprehend her brother's death...

"You've seen the basement, right? Well, there's another entrance. My dad doesn't think I know about it, but this is where he keeps his best wines." Chloe led Kathi Jo to a large walk-in pantry connected to the kitchen.

"I really need to go," Kathi Jo said. There was nothing she wanted more now than to get away from Chloe, her sadness. *Her madness.*

"One drink. We'll toast to my brother. To his memory," Chloe said.

Kathi Jo didn't have the heart to tell her now, about how she had tried to end things with Blake. It seemed like a selfish thing to confess right now anyway.

"Help me move this," Chloe said. There was a long metal shelf filled with cleaning supplies and old rags.

"But it will fall," Kathi Jo protested.

"Oh, who cares if it does? My brother is dead! Take off that silly coat. You look like a pink flamingo. I always hated that coat. Roll your sleeves up and help me," Chloe grunted, tugging on one side of the shelf.

Kathi Jo slipped the coat off, dropping it to the floor with a clatter, then she went to the other end of the shelf. Chloe pulled and Kathi Jo pushed, the shelf scraping noisily as it scooted across the linoleum. As the shelf slid away from the wall, a door behind it was revealed. It looked like a normal door, another entrance to the basement as Chloe had claimed. But the door was heavy and thick with metal.

"It's locked," Kathi Jo said, turning the knob.

"Good thing I have a key," Chloe grinned. The key was tucked in the front of her trousers. She took it out and held it up, proudly. It looked like one of those old skeleton keys. Kathi Jo had never seen anything like it.

"I'm sorry about Blake, Chloe. I'm so sad he's gone … but I need to go now."

"Go where? It looks to me like you're running away," Chloe said, pointing at Kathi Jo's backpack on the floor. "Just one drink, okay?"

Chloe slipped the key in the lock and turned it. The door creaked open loudly. Inside, there were a pair of steps leading down into what looked like a dank dark hole.

"I'm the only one with the key. Can you believe it? When my parents bought this place, they said there was no key to it … but I found it one day, under the floorboard in one of the guest rooms. I should have told them I found it, but what's the fun in that? I like being the only one—"

"But I thought you said your dad kept his wines down here?" Kathi Jo said, staring down into the darkness. *There was no way in hell she was going down there. No fucking way.*

"I guess you're not the only one who tells lies," Chloe said, wriggling her eyebrows.

"I don't understand…" Kathi Jo said, trying to back away from the door.

But Chloe had her trapped, blocking her from moving away.

"It's cold down there. You might want your stupid coat." Chloe reached down and snatched it up off the floor. "I saw it, you know. On the floor of another place. At my dad's apartment, to be exact. I could hear you all back there in his room."

"What? No, Chloe! The only time I've been to your dad's was with Blake," Kathi Jo said, breathlessly.

"You fucked my dad, and then what? Killed my brother because he found out? You deserved what he did to you, bitch! I saw the bruises. You're a stupid little whore."

"Chloe, I didn't… I wouldn't…" Kathi Jo pleaded.

"Don't worry. You'll have a long time to make amends," Chloe said.

"What? No! I'm sorry... I didn't..."

"I would say, 'I hope you rot in hell', but what's the point? I already know you will," Chloe said.

Chloe pressed a firm hand on Kathi Jo's lower back and shoved her into the dark, yawning hole.

Chapter Twenty-One

A VIOLENT END

CURRENT DAY

"I think it used to be a bunker," Chloe said.

I watched her, tugging on the old metal shelf, a deep-seeded sense of terror growing deep inside me. *What is she about to show me?*

The gun was gone, clattered to the floor in the living room and useless to me now.

Who was I kidding? The gun was always useless.

"After World War I, the military built them. Wealthy families did, too. Small and soundproof, the idea was to protect yourself from air raids or bombs. That's why I knew it'd be perfect. And I'm the only one with the key. Always have been." Chloe beamed.

She was sweaty and breathing in excited pants as she revealed the plain white door behind the shelf. I watched, holding my own breath, as she took out an old key and inserted it in the lock.

I should turn around and run. But I need to know what happened to my friend.

"Go on. She's down there," Chloe told me.

"You first," I said, voice shaky with fear.

"Fine… You're still no fun, Willow." Chloe stepped down in the dark. There were nearly a dozen concrete steps, the air below cool and airless like a vacuum.

"Do you know how long it takes to die of starvation? Not as long as you might think. She was gone in less than ten days. I made myself wait ten days; you see, I wanted to delay the pleasure. But by the time I came down here, she was already gone. Ewww… I haven't been down here in a few years. She's really lost her figure."

From the center of the staircase, I could already see her. Or what used to be Kathi Jo. She looked tiny, a small, fossilized mound on the floor, strings of hair and cloth molded to her bones.

"No, it's not her … please…" I begged.

Chloe squatted down next to the pile of bone matter. Then she held up Kathi Jo's backpack and the fleecy pink jacket I returned to her the night of Blake's fall decades ago.

"Oh God…" I could feel myself slipping, losing

consciousness in the damp, dark room. My hand was slipping on the rail and as I tried to stop myself from falling, I scratched at the cold hard walls in the stairwell. But I was tumbling, falling into the darkness. To join my long-lost friend.

Chapter Twenty-Two

A CINDERELLA STORY

CURRENT DAY

I don't think I'm what my Grandma Minnie had in mind when she pressured my mother to name me after a Disney princess.

Whether it was the name itself or just the way I was born, I always resented it—even when I was little, and my classmates were jealous of it. The older I got, the more they teased, and by middle grade I'd shortened my name to Cindy.

I'd always been opposed to all things girly—dresses and bows, even typical career paths my mother tried to choose for me. I did poorly in school, not because I was stupid but because all the subjects bored me. I liked working with my hands, taking things apart and putting them back together. Working in construction wasn't a means to an end for me—it was my passion, the only thing I enjoyed doing these days.

Although I had hoped to one day run my own crew, for now I had settled on working for Mack.

I lied when I told Willow I was married. Not because I'm gay—although every bastard I meet assumes that. But because I enjoy my own company over anyone else's. The excuse about having a row with a husband was the best I could come up with on the fly. I hadn't expected her to ask, seeing as that there was a "dead body" in the closet of her lake house.

I grew up on a farm in Montana, far away from my cousin, Kathi Jo, and my mother's sister, Isabella. I met them once or twice when I was younger, but truthfully, I don't even remember that now.

But after Kathi Jo ran away, that all changed… Isabella came to stay with us that year. It was supposed to be temporary, but she never left. And when my mother got diagnosed with breast cancer the very next year, Aunt Isabella stayed on to look after me. When my mama died, Isabella became like a second mother. Dare I say I loved her just as much as my own, after we both got used to each other.

It was a strange partnership, her losing her daughter and me, my mother—we were two lost souls with nothing to cling to but each other.

The cancer that killed her sister finally reached her too, so I made her a promise on her deathbed. A promise that someday, I would find out the truth about Kathi Jo. I would track her down for Isabella.

I think Isabella held out hope for the impossible, that Kathi Jo was alive and well out there somewhere. But I knew better. In the age of social media, it's damn near impossible for people to remain hidden forever.

Kathi Jo didn't go missing. Someone in Hillendale made her disappear.

The first two years living here and working for Mack, I made no progress. I searched everywhere, the old grounds and the woods. I even invested in expensive sonar and scoured the lake under the guise of fishing, going so far as to put on a wetsuit and deep dive, looking for her myself in my free time.

But Kathi Jo was nowhere to be found, which meant *someone* had her. *Someone* knew the truth.

As I talked to Aunt Isabella throughout the years, one name kept coming up over and over—Kathi Jo's best friend and summertime next-door neighbor, Willow Roberts. And when I learned that Willow had inherited the lake house and was returning to Hillendale, it felt like fate.

I used the last of my paycheck to purchase the fake corpse; I thought I'd be able to determine her guilt based on her reaction, but it only confused me further. She seemed genuinely upset and seemed to truly believe it was Kathi Jo's body in the closet. And she didn't discover the note I'd written until later.

But I still wasn't completely convinced of her innocence. So, that's why I installed the camera.

There was enough time to install a good-sized trail camera on the tree outside, but I'd been interrupted by Willow herself when I was inside trying to hide three nest cams in the house.

Tonight, the house was dark with no one around. I left my truck parked at the corner and walked through the shadows toward the lake house. The trail cam was camouflaged and hidden fairly well by the foliage of the oak tree out front. I gathered it quickly and rushed back to my truck, praying Willow didn't decide to sneak in through the back and catch me off guard again.

Back in my truck, I carefully removed the SD card from the camera and booted up my laptop. I was eager to review the most recent footage but unsure what I expected to find. Ideally, Willow Roberts doing something suspect, something that could lead me to my cousin's body, or convince me she knew more than she was letting on.

The rumor mill in Hillendale claimed that Willow was attacked last night—*if true, I should be able to see something. And if she made it up, well then, that is important to know too.*

But right away, I found the culprit. A stranger moving

through the shadows. The footage was a little grainy, but I could see a dark, hooded figure approaching the lake house, just as Willow had claimed.

"Damn." They weren't close enough to the camera to make out a face, though.

Then, moments later, there was someone else—Trevor McDonald. He was running through the yard, straight toward the house. I froze the footage again and rewound. Watching the hooded figure, followed by Trevor's fast-moving, panicked approach. I didn't know Trevor too well—a local man who was familiar with my cousin, but I'd never truly suspected his involvement.

I hit play and let the footage keep rolling. Suddenly, the hooded figure was back. Running for his or her life, stumbling right past the tree as Trevor chased them off.

"There you are." I clicked the pause button and backed up a couple seconds. And there was the flash of a face, clear and frightened, only meters away from the camera hidden in the tree. I froze on the guilty party's face and zoomed in.

Chloe Ashcroft. Everyone in Hillendale knew the Ashcrofts, and Chloe was known as a pretentious bitch. But I'd never expected her to be involved in something like this...

I put the truck in gear and took out my phone, doing what I should have done last night when I heard about the attack on Willow. I should have admitted to the police that I had a camera trained on the lake house, that I could help with their investigation, but I hadn't wanted to get in trouble for what I'd done either.

The fake dummy, the note, the camera … it wasn't murder, but it certainly was some sort of felony. The last thing I wanted to do was lose my job with Mack.

Did Chloe have something to do with my cousin's disappearance? She must have if she was sneaking around the lake house and trying to scare Willow out of town.

"Officer Beckham speaking," a voice huffed into my ear. I steered the truck wildly through the streets of Hillendale, telling her everything through labored breaths.

When I parked in front of the Ashcroft manor, Willow's car was there waiting, parked but empty in the driveway.

I arrived just before the police did, and within the hour, I would watch as they carried my poor dear cousin's final remains out the front door of her murderer's home.

I found her, Isabella. Not in the way you wanted her to be found, but I'm bringing her home to you soon.

Epilogue

I fell into Cindy's arms that day, unable to watch as they escorted Chloe Ashcroft out of the Ashcroft lake house, in handcuffs. Later, the hospice would come to retrieve Ian Ashcroft from his room upstairs ... but I didn't wait around for that part either.

I didn't know Cindy, but I let her hold me that day. And she let me hold her back, too. She was the closest, and the only, connection I had left to Kathi Jo. When she explained who she was and apologized for the mannequin and the note, I instantly forgave her. After all, Kat's blood was running through her veins.

Weeks later, as I stood at Kathi Jo's memorial marker, I had to wonder if I ever really knew her. I mean, we were friends—the best of friends—for only a few summers. There was the girl from that summer, and then there was this living legend in my mind ... the best friend that no one else could ever measure up to. In my mind, my memories, she is the best that ever will be. I don't care if it's true or exaggerated anymore; for a while, we had the best of both worlds—caught between being a child and an adult, walking the dangerous tightrope between the two.

Those summers were magic and tragic: the only time when I really let my guard down and trusted someone else enough to let them see the real me ... and the only time my heart felt so destroyed that for a while I couldn't go on.

Cindy eventually returned to Montana, but we promised to stay in touch. She took Kathi Jo's remains back with her—she belonged with her mother's remains; Isabella would have wanted that.

I returned the key to the apartment to Bart, but I took Smokey with me when I went. She absolutely hated the car ride, meowing relentlessly and scratching at the bars of the cat carrier, but luckily, we didn't have too far to go. It's a short ride to the other side of the lake.

The lake house belongs to me now. It isn't perfect, but I'm determined to make it mine—a new home, blanketed with old memories. I replaced the empty spots where the animal heads once were with pictures that made me smile. Pictures of Grandma Lucy and Dad at the lake when Dad was a little boy. Pics of my mom and dad when they were young, happy, and carefree. And a few snapshots of me and Kathi Jo, too.

I invited Sydney and her family to come to the lake house. I didn't expect her to come, but then she started showing up every weekend. Sometimes she brought the whole family, and other times it was just her and the girls. I learned to make the girls' favorite foods—hotdogs with beans (beanie weenies they called them) and peanut butter and banana sandwiches. I rented an old pontoon boat and took the girls out on the lake. Sydney and I strapped them into life jackets and let them float around like turtles in the water, paddling and squealing with delight.

Tommy came up occasionally and one weekend, he even taught me to fly fish. There was an art to it; it required patience and skill I hadn't realized I had in me. It made me happy—making new memories on the lake. I liked this older version of him; this older version of *us*.

Trevor relapsed shortly after Chloe's trial. I don't see him often, but occasionally, he appears on the Hillendale streets, passing me like a ghost who doesn't recognize— or perhaps, doesn't want to—his former friends.

There's not a day that goes by that I don't think about what Kathi Jo went through and wonder at the horrors of what she experienced at the end. I think about choices. What I could have done differently.

I think about how much I miss her.

There are times when I see Blake's face, falling in the dark. *Down, down, down …* that look of shock in his eyes, the flash of betrayal. Sometimes the face changes, distorted in my dreams. His face turns into Ian's, twisted and tortured, then it changes to my ex-husband, Jason, too. Sometimes it's her I see, my best friend falling. I have nightmares that I pushed her off that tower. I didn't, but still, the moment I sealed Blake's fate I sealed Kathi Jo's too. Chloe wouldn't have killed her if it hadn't been for me. I know I'm responsible for many things … and there are secrets I'll take with me to the grave. But I can't turn back now; I can't undo what's already done.

At my old teaching job, I was surrounded by colleagues who were friends with my shitty ex-husband. Here, in a place that feels so old and familiar, I'll get a fresh start where no one knows me at Hillendale Middle School.

Since I never went to school here, I'm not familiar with the halls or the teachers, or any of the local parents, either. Here, I'm safe to get back to what I love doing: teaching and working with kids.

I used to want to work with the little ones—they're cute during the primary years and their brains are so soft and malleable. They soak up information like little sponges. But it is those in-between years that matter most, I think. That is when shit hits the fan, as Kathi Jo used to say, that is when they lose their spark.

I want to work with kids who were our age—the age when we lost it all. The dividing line between beauty and danger is never greater than when we are young.

Here, at Hillendale Middle School, there is one face I recognize—but it's destined for the memory wall. Kathi Jo, her middle school class pictures and photos of her swimming team. She looked happy then. She looks like the girl I remember.

Somehow, I want to get back to the girl I remember in myself. The one who believed in magic; the one who believed that the power of creative thinking could solve anything.

Kathi Jo's memory isn't a stain on this town, it's a blanket. She's here to remind me that good friends come once in a lifetime, and we rarely get to keep them for long. All that truly remain are the memories.

Acknowledgments

I am forever grateful to my editor, Jennie Rothwell, for supporting my writing. Thank you for making me a better writer and for believing in me. Thank you to Tony Russell and Federica Leonardis for you invaluable help during the copyedits and proofreading stages. Thank you to all of the staff at One More Chapter and HarperCollins for working tirelessly behind the scenes and in front of the scenes to get my books in the hands of readers all over the world.

Huge thanks to my brilliant literary agent, Katie Shea Boutillier, and the Donald Maass Literary Agency, for supporting me every step of the way and being my biggest cheerleaders!

Thank you to my family and friends for loving me just the way I am…

Thank you to my fluffy kitty, Kai, who can't read but probably wishes she could. Kai kept her paws on the back of my shoulders for at least 50% of the process, while writing this book. Thanks for the support, Kai!

To Ginger, my sweet friend. You were the BEST

FRIEND a girl could ask for. I will miss you forever and ever. Rest In Peace, dear heart.

Last but not least, thank you to YOU, dear reader, for taking a chance on my books! Please leave me a review and let me know what you think.

Extract Sample : The Bachelorette Party

Prologue

Crime Scene, Walkthrough #1

The detective walks through a tunnel of weepy oak trees, follows the picturesque path to the glowing French doors. She tries to imagine herself in the killer's shoes.

Did the killer sneak up on them? Or were they already inside when the party started?

She stares up at the strange, eclectic house. It inspires awe and horror in tandem.

The pediments and classic columns give the place an undeniable Greek feel. But like so many other domiciles in New Orleans, it's a haunting patchwork of influence—the Spanish and Caribbean flashes of color and design;

the Creole parapets and cast-iron balconies; the Victorian motifs twisted like lace. And the siding looks Italian...

A true work of architectural genius... too bad its reputation will be tainted after today, the detective thinks.

Someone has decorated the front of the house, either for the event or a leftover from Mardi Gras, gaudy swoops of pearls and flowers ... and massive bride and groom statues, which look to be made of paper mâché, keep watch at the carriageway.

The detective stares at their faces; stoic, they reveal nothing about what transpired here. *What secrets are you hiding?* she wonders.

Through the carriageway, she stops at the French doors. Her assistant helps her into boot covers and gloves. He tucks her long dark hair into a rubbery hairnet.

The assistant is young and male, barely twenty. His eyes are frightened. His skin has turned a muted gray. But the detective pretends not to notice.

"Take me to her, please," she says.

Down a marbled hallway lined with a dark mix of Parisian and contemporary paintings, the assistant stops at the entry of a grand dining room and points. It's large enough to fit a ballroom inside it.

On a long wooden table are the remnants of half-eaten food. The pungent aroma of rotting oysters fills the air. There are open wine bottles scattered from the head of the table on down.

The banquet takes up a substantial portion of the room, but the centerpiece of the space ... at the centerpiece is the woman.

The detective moves in, tiptoeing like a ghoulish ballet dancer around the ghastly main attraction.

The noose is tight around the victim's neck. She dangles from the rafter, still as a statue carved by Marcus Aurelius himself, as though she's part of the mishmash design that comes with the house, with this entire city...

The victim's eyes are open, staring.

The detective turns, follows her gaze toward the putrid food spread, trying to see through her victim's eyes. *What was the last thing you saw before you died? Or should I say:* who *did you see?*

There are others in the room—technicians, scouring for clues—but the detective might as well be alone with the dead woman. *What happened to you?* the detective wonders, eyes combing the woman's body for answers. Hanging there, still and stoic, she looks weightless...

Why did someone do this to you? And most importantly— who hated you enough to kill?

The detective walks a full circle around the victim, eyes never leaving the body. She nearly steps in a small puddle of blood before the assistant stops her.

Kneeling, she examines the coin-shaped blot on the marble floor, glancing back up at the victim.

The victim wears a long white dress, nearly see-through. No shoes. Her toenails are painted hot pink.

The detective cannot say for certain until the medical examiner arrives, but she doesn't think the victim died by hanging.

"What are you thinking?" the assistant asks, mustering some stoicism despite his sickly pallor.

"Well, I can't say for sure. But I don't see much injury around the ligature. No scratch marks ... and she doesn't appear to have clawed at the noose. If someone strung you up like that, you'd fight like hell, wouldn't you?"

The assistant's face turns ashier.

"Maybe the victim put herself up there," he squeaks.

The detective shakes her head, slowly considering.

"Not a chance," she says, finally.

"Well, how do you know?"

The detective lifts an arm, points a latex finger at the back of the victim's head. "Can't see it too clearly from here, but she suffered from a head injury there on the back of her skull. The blood on the floor probably came from her, but this isn't where she was hit. A wound like that ... it would have caused a whole lot of mess...and I don't think the victim hit herself in the back of the head before hanging, do you? And how did she get herself up there? There's no stool or chair nearby..." The detective is talking at him, but she's mostly talking it through with herself.

She motions for one of the technicians and points at the blood on the floor.

Later, as the body is cut down and removed, the detective roams the halls of the mansion, room by room, taking it all in. She has had no luck finding a weapon.

A blow like that would have come from something hard ... and from someone with a fast swing, she thinks, inquisitively.

The detective imagines the perpetrator, lifting something heavy over the victim's head. She sees the weight of the blow ... hears the whale-like moan someone might make after sustaining a sudden brain injury of that nature.

The detective's lieutenant has passed along some details already, but she wants to walk it through herself a few more times. She needs to get a feel of this place ... needs to know what happened, and how a joyous night could turn out so devastating. So tragic ... so grisly.

Six women were present at the party and now one of them is dead.

The remaining five are in custody, secured and separated at the scene, and now awaiting questions down at the station. *Hopefully being managed with care until we have more information*, the detective thinks to herself.

The detective stops in the doorway of a massive library. Floor to ceiling shelves are crammed with heavy volumes and tomes. She has an eye for order and prides herself for it. *Whoever the caretaker of this place might be, they certainly have an eye for order too,* she realizes.

The books are organized by height and width, the thickest and tallest volumes on the left, cascading from left to right, growing thinner and shorter, all the way to the smallest and narrowest volumes. It flows seamlessly ... *perfectly.*

The detective's eyes roam the spines, left to right then down a row, right to left ... it takes her less than a minute to find it—the chaos commingling with the order.

The offender is a thick red tome inched between two narrow tomes of the same height.

As she removes it, slowly and with care, she realizes the book isn't red at all. Rather, it is meant to be brown, but something has stained the corner of the heavy paperboard binding and leaked down the sides of it.

The detective turns it over and back, stares at the thick clump of hair and scalp attached to the sharpest edge. Her body jolts with surprise and revulsion.

"I need help from someone in here," she whisper-shouts, hands shaky from the weight of the book, and the horror of what has happened here.

The detective's voice booms around the cavernous space, echoing back in her face. *This place feels less like a historical monument and more like an ill-fated tomb,* she thinks, hairs rising on the back of her neck for the first time all night.

Earlier, the detective saw pictures of the women—a fun-filled weekend; a celebration of what should have been one of the best moments in life…an event catalogued in real time with the help of social media and social influence…

But all the filters in the world can't hide this sort of darkness.

They could cover up their flaws and grievances with Gingham or Valencia filters, but no amount of lighting or special effects could change what one of them has done…

A monster in a pretty dress is still a monster.

PART I
A little party never killed nobody. - Fergie

Chapter One

ROSALEE

The bride-to-be

The backyard of our new home spread before me, stretching over a gentle slope then unfolding into a pasture. Beyond that, the land melted into a quiet hush of sugar maple trees and smudgy, rolling hills in every direction.

Two mares stood in the pasture, silent and watchful, unbothered by the eerie hush of falling snow. I stood at the edge of our veranda, weightless snowflakes brushing my cheeks and hands. I wondered if the horses were sleeping… *Do horses stand when they sleep or lie down?*

The smell of manure was strong, despite the cold, but

the odor didn't bother me. The realtor had warned us when we walked the place, but the pasture smelled just fine to me—like farmland and fresh air. Like a fresh start for my tiny two-person family...

Asher and I had lived here for nearly a month now, but still, I hadn't adjusted. Half our belongings were still stowed away in boxes, pushed aside in the deep dark corners of our three-bedroom farmhouse.

It's perfect, Asher told the real estate agent, before turning to me. *Isn't it perfect, Rosalee?*

What else could I say but "yes", in that moment? I loved the farmhouse; this was true. And the way Asher's eyes lit up when he was excited about something, whether it was a big case he was working on at the law firm, or a story he read online...his eyes, warm and brown like pecans, would grow smiley and wide, like a kid bubbling over with Christmas morning delight.

Later, as the real estate agent typed up the deal, he repeated those words: *It's perfect.* Adding this: *For now.*

Us and a couple of kids. The perfect place to raise a family. Until we want to have even more kids, and we eventually outgrow the place, he had said.

I shivered at the memory. Yes, the house was perfect, and I loved my fiancé, but the thought of having so many kids we would soon outgrow it? *Not in the plans for me.*

I loved the solitude of Moon County. The earthiness of dirt and manure. You could drive from one side of town to the other in 30 minutes, counting the crows and telephone wires … pointing out the silos and family farms that had obviously been around for generations. One generation gives way to the next … a bunch of knock-offs walking around, replacing the youth that came before them. We're all different here, yet all the same.

I love it here, but also—I don't feel settled. Not yet.

"You're freezing." Asher wrapped his thick arms around me from behind, squeezing me close to his chest. He smelled like aftershave and his favorite coffee, an over-priced bourbon barrel-aged brew. He was wearing his thick, black terrycloth robe. But still, I could feel his erection as he held me close. I shivered and pressed up against him.

"It seems wrong to go," I whispered, icy words forming foggy little puffs around my head. "We're just getting settled...and this is our first snow since moving..." Asher squeezed tighter, too tight … and I tried to relax, giving into the curve of his body, a shudder of pleasure running through me.

I didn't want to leave Asher—we hadn't spent a night apart from one another in ages.

～

I developed a crush on him in middle school, but then I had to move away. It wasn't until I came back to Moon County that we had our first "real" connection. But for me, my feelings for Asher had been going on for as long as I had hormones to act on. Even now, at twenty-eight, it felt surreal to think we were together. *We are getting married soon. Who would have thought?*

Perhaps that could account for the unsettled lump in my chest … *We're not married yet. He could still back out,* that vile voice of self-doubt in my brain.

Asher laughed, a thick rumble in his chest that vibrated through me and turned my body warm all over. *He has the best laugh. He might not be perfect, but that laugh … it's one of his best features. Always has been.*

"Who are you kidding, Rosalee? You hate the snow."

True. Although he doesn't exactly know why. Talk of my parents' fatal accident was something I avoided whenever possible, even with my future husband.

For me, the beauty of snow will always be intertwined with those ugly, dark days of death. That haunting silence snow brings…as though the entire world is vacuum-sealed and there's no one around to save you…

"And," Asher continued, "there's not that much left to unpack." *Lie.* The thought of all those boxes and all the sorting that needed doing … it overwhelmed all of my senses, the pressure thick in my chest to just *get it done, get it done...*

"What will you do without me though? You'll be lonely," I teased, my mood changing. I turned around, wrapping my arms around his waist, then lifting up on my toes to kiss him. Even first thing in the morning, the milky-sweetness of his skin and lips was enticing.

He rocked back on his heels playfully, then squeezed my face in his hands.

"Ah. Don't you worry about me. I have work to do on the Werner file and in my free time, I'll probably get drunk on cheap beer and start hanging some of your art on the walls," he grinned.

I groaned but smiled, unable to contain my pleasure. I wanted a place to hang my art pieces too, but if Asher had it his way, they'd be displayed front and center—in the living room or foyer, for all of our guests to see. I liked that he was proud of my work, but it also embarrassed me.

"Don't you dare. Wait until I come back at least," I said, taking my last longing glance toward the pasture. The horses were gone now, as though they'd never been there to begin with. My eyes drifted over to the gazebo next to the farmhouse; bright blue with tiny white pockets of flowers on its beams, it was one of my favorite features on the property.

I had suggested, casually, that perhaps we should

hold the wedding here, in the gazebo. A simple ceremony on our lovely new patch of land...

Of course, Asher's mother nearly choked on her biscuit when I said that. "She's teasing, Mom. Relax," Asher had said, rubbing smooth circles over his mother Elizabeth's back until her throat cleared.

"Well, I sure hope so. I've paid a fortune for Merribelle Gardens and already paid countless deposits on the flowers and caterers," she had huffed, refusing to meet my eye as she dabbled her lips with a fancy white linen napkin. That day, we had met for lunch at her favorite restaurant—a snobby, upscale place that charged 100 dollars for a dab of meat with a smear of potatoes and a lettuce leaf on it.

I'd been horrified by it, even if she were the one paying the tab.

Ah yes—the grand Merribelle Gardens, the destination for our wedding this October.

Merribelle Gardens and all the money my future mother-in-law had so generously put forth for our wedding. The whole grand plan had been her idea—a *tradition*, since she and Asher's late father had been married there in 1972.

I'd seen the glamorous pictures of their wedding day, countless times. Elizabeth in her big ballgown with its floaty A-line and mother-of-pearl buttons ... she had looked like a movie star. And Asher's father—tall and demure in his fancy black waistcoat with its classic pocket square.

There was no way Asher and I could live up to his mother's ideal wedding tradition.

It wasn't that I was opposed to getting married there. It's just … I couldn't shake off the feeling that it was being held over my head; a constant reminder that I should feel grateful, *indebted*, to the Beake family, for simply letting me be a part of it.

My own parents weren't around to help pay for the wedding, and even if they had been, they were never as well off as Asher's family.

Whenever Elizabeth discussed the upcoming wedding, I often felt guilty, as though no matter how much I thanked her for planning and paying for it, and no matter how much enthusiasm I tried to muster, none of it was good enough. I suspected that she didn't like me. Dare I say, even hated me.

And all of my suggestions and ideas for the wedding were pushed aside … *how dare the peasant bride have an opinion, right?!*

I wasn't joking that day at the restaurant when I suggested the gazebo. I did love our new farmhouse … and the thought of having a small ceremony in my own mother's plain white dress with feet bare was appealing.

But I didn't want to disappoint Asher, and I certainly didn't want to disappoint his overly critical mother.

"Hey. Don't worry. Go! Have fun. You deserve this weekend. It's yours to celebrate," Asher said, shaking me out of my worried thoughts.

"Okay. If you insist," I sighed. Although, he and I both knew, there was no way of getting out of New Orleans either. My best friend Mara had planned the bachelorette party; like Elizabeth, Mara wasn't opposed to using guilt and pressure to get her way.

Truthfully, I was excited to hang out with Mara. And the others ... mostly. I'd never been to New Orleans and the thought of celebrating for a few days with friends in an authentic Greek Revival in the Garden District was too exotic to resist. It would be nice to get away for a few days ... from the mess and stress of packing. From the wedding jitters and constant questions and answers from the wedding planners...

I needed a break from it all. The engagement, the home-buying process, the move ... it was all too much for my historically fragile mental health.

Asher led me in through the back door, nudging me towards our bedroom to pack for the trip. "I'll make coffee and eggs. Maybe some pork sausage..." Even though the man worked ungodly hours at the law firm, he was a phenom in the kitchen when he offered to cook.

"Sounds wonderful." I kissed his cheek and drifted off to our room. My suitcase was under the bed, old and mostly unused. It had been years since I'd travelled anywhere.

Humming softly, I filled the soft fabric lining of the case with pockets of panties and bras, and my best t-shirts and jeans that had been unpacked. Despite the chilly weather here, the forecast in Louisiana looked perfect—a balmy 79 degrees. I tossed in pajamas and a couple old bathing suits in case there was a pool. I was tempted to try them on to see if they still fit, but then I'd get depressed about my weight gain ... over the last couple years, I'd put on nearly twenty pounds. Being in love and going out to eat all the time with your fiancé will do that, I guess. But it didn't make me feel very good when I tried to squeeze into undergarments or swimwear.

I'll just deal with trying on bathing suits when I get there, I decided, hastily.

After my clothes were all packed, I went in search of my tickets. They were in a folder, tucked away with all the airline details printed out by Mara and my cousin, Tinsley.

Where's that folder now, then? I wondered.

As I wandered down the hall to Asher's office, I could hear the sizzle of sausages and smell the warm scent of toast and coffee. My stomach grumbled.

Asher's office was still a work in progress, like the rest of the house. Housed in one of the spare bedrooms, he had a single desk and chair. The desktop was littered with files and folders. I spotted the neon yellow folder with my flight itinerary in it, balanced on a crooked stack of papers on the corner of the desk. He had obviously moved the folder into his office, thinking it was one of his.

I scooped up the folder and opened it, double checking my flight time and that everything I needed was there. Glancing at the other stack of papers on his desk, I was reminded of all the paperwork and drama that had been involved in buying our new, and first, home together.

Copies of our bank statements, tax forms, and every single asset we had ever owned … the only thing the mortgage lender didn't ask for was a picture of the inside of my underwear drawer…

I need to go through these papers when I get back, file away the important ones and shred the duplicates…

I picked up the stack in my hands and straightened it, then set it back down neatly on the desk. I was about to turn away with my folder in hand, when my eyes drifted to a line item I hadn't noticed before on the top sheet of one of our bank statements.

Truthfully, I'd barely paid any of it any mind, just printing and printing and printing whatever the mortgage lender asked for.

Now, I picked the statement up, studying one of the

bank charges listed at the very top. A recurring membership charge. For a place I knew all too well. A place Asher had no business going to…

In the kitchen, I held the folder to my chest like a shield, watching the man I loved making breakfast. He glanced up at me and smiled, wagging the spatula playfully.

When I closed my eyes, I could see us there—on our first date. I'd always been intimidated by him as a young kid … his family's money, his confidence, his popularity, and his intimidating social circle. But then I ran into him a local art fair, and the second he saw me, he waved and came strolling over, much to my surprise. *Rosalee, right? Long time, no see!* I was shocked that he remembered my name. We stood there in the park for an hour, leaning between rows of local artisans' tents, just talking. He spoke passionately about his law practice, but he wasn't one of those guys—like I had expected—who centered the conversation around himself. He asked questions about my life away from Moon County, about my art degree, my interests … a week later, he tracked me down on Facebook and asked me out on a proper date. I'd expected something classic, a fancy dinner or a trip to the local movie theater to see the new James Bond. But he surprised me with tickets to an art gallery in a neighboring city. He had seemed so thoughtful, so unexpectedly humble and kind … and over the years, his loyalty to me never seemed to waver.

Asher was my dream guy, not just his looks but his personality too. He was confident but caring, and he seemed to adore me. *That's why finding that bank charge makes no sense…*

I watched my future husband dance around the kitchen, preparing my breakfast, wondering if I'd been wrong about him all along.

I thought I could trust him with my life, but perhaps that's not the case…

Chapter Two

ELIZABETH

The mother-in-law

"Are you sure about this? It's not too late to switch flights."

"Mom, stop it." My daughter, Bri, jabbed an elbow in my rib cage, but she was smiling when she did it. I knew she wanted to be here about as much as I did.

"Seriously. I have miles on my Amex. We could go anywhere you want. The Galapagos. Or, hey, what about Paris?" I teased.

I adjusted the backs of my diamond earrings, patted my neatly coifed bun. I was getting old, sure, my hair thinning and white, and my skin wrinkled as a prune, but I always strived to look my best, wearing expensive clothes in muted colors, and visiting my stylist once a month. *I refuse to be one of those lazy old women ... walking around in a housedress and rollers.*

"There she is," Bri spoke from the corner of her mouth, dipping her head toward my future daughter-in-law, Rosalee.

Rosalee stumbled through the terminal, catching herself just in time. She had a dented old suitcase swaying at her side.

"Good lord. Is that all she brought with her, that tiny suitcase?"

Bri's lips tightened; her thick brows furrowed together. "Looks like it, mom."

I felt for her, Bri's baby brother getting married when, in reality, it should have been her.

My daughter was beautiful, but different. Bri had her father's stature and face, his squarish jaw and thick, broad shoulders. And when she was angry, she looked like a linebacker perched for attack on the field. As much as I had wanted it for her—marriage, babies, a traditional life ... it wasn't her thing. She was focused on her career, building computers and creating her own custom models. I didn't understand a bit of it, but I always told myself I was proud of her. Even if I had to remind myself of it from time to time...

I am proud of my daughter, even if she doesn't choose to live her life the way I expected her to.

I zeroed in on my clumsy daughter-in-law-to-be as she stopped in front of us. She dropped her suitcase at her feet and tugged on her stubby black ponytail, a line of sweat beading at her brow. *How can someone so young look so sweaty and out-of-breath all the time?* I wondered, and not for the first time.

"I went to the wrong terminal. And then I got hassled at security over the buckles on my shoes," Rosalee breathed.

Glancing down at her feet, I was horrified to see a pair of cheap Payless shoes that looked like a carryover from the nineties.

"They're comfortable," Rosalee said, following my gaze. "My mom always said to dress comfortably while traveling." She shrugged, then chewed her bottom lip— one awful habit out of many.

But I did feel a small lurch in my chest at the mention of her mother. *It could not have been easy, losing her mother and father at such an early age. But surely ... her mother could have taught her a thing or two about fashion, about walking with her head up and finding a sense of direction ... about not wearing such ridiculous shoes...*

Standing next to Bri and me, with our designer bags and expensive, yet *still comfortable*, shoes, Rosalee looked plumb ridiculous. I'd never been a flashy dresser—

dressing like a Vegas showgirl isn't necessary for displaying wealth. But I liked classic designs and pantsuits…

I bet Rosalee doesn't even own a nice pantsuit or dress shoes … how does she plan to attend dinners with Asher, when he meets with clients and colleagues, if she doesn't have a decent set of shoes?!

"Oh, I almost forgot! Here's your shirt." Bri beamed, as she thrust a folded pink t-shirt into Rosalee's hands. The words "The Future Mrs. Beake" were embroidered in hideous sparkly gold letters on the front of it.

I couldn't help smiling as I watched Rosalee unfold the shirt and hold it up to her face. There was a flicker of something—a tiny clench in her jaw. But then she smiled brightly at Bri. "I love it! Thank you so much for making the shirts, Bri."

That flicker of annoyance, quickly masked with gratitude, came as no surprise to me. Rosalee's best friend and maid of honor, Mara, and her cousin, Tinsley, were in charge of throwing the bachelorette party. Yet my daughter Bri had insisted on overseeing the shirts from Day One. Bri had a close friend from high school who designed her own t-shirts—a cheesy endeavor, if you ask me—and she had promised to get them well made, and at a reasonable price. But the others should have known … price isn't really something we worry about.

Mara had suggested something cute and classy—

"Here comes the bride", "Crown me"—and even a few funny inscriptions—"Bride-zilla", "Soon to be under new management". But I was the one who pushed for "The Future Mrs. Beake", and Bri had gone along with it too. *She always listens to her mother.*

It's not my fault Rosalee wants to keep her own last name. Disgraceful, that's what it is. She should be grateful to call herself a Beake now, especially considering the social standing the name will give her...

I'd expected an angrier reaction from her when she saw the shirt, but I should have known better—Rosalee was polite, if anything. Always biting her lip, being a try-hard when it came to impressing us and Asher. But I could see through her phony routine.

I watched in horror as Rosalee removed her thin jacket and started tugging the new t-shirt over the ratty one she was already wearing.

"Oh, you don't have to do that now..." Bri said, looking around at passersby, embarrassed.

"No, I want to! Thanks again for this. I just adore it. Your friend who makes these is very talented," Rosalee beamed, struggling to pull the t-shirt over her breasts and flabby stomach. She wasn't a heavy girl, but she certainly wasn't in shape. Last year I bought her a pair of maternity pants for Christmas, hoping she would take the hint. Instead, she had thanked me and promised to wear them soon.

Knowing her and her fashion sense, she probably does wear them...

"Where are the others?" I sniffed, looking at my favorite watch with its diamond band. It was a present from Edmund on our twenty-fifth anniversary. I blinked back memories of that day, his cheesy grin, slipping the velvet box across the table before I'd even taken a bite of my dinner. He'd always been so impatient when it came to gift-giving. He loved the thrill of seeing me open things; watching my eyes sparkle at the presents he bestowed upon me. Despite all his showiness and spoils, he was never a man who cared about buying things for himself. His favorite thing to wear was holey pajama pants and he didn't even own any jewelry. *Edmund probably would have loved Rosalee,* I thought, a flicker of annoyance running down my spine as I continued to watch her struggle with the too-tight shirt.

"Georgia's almost here. Not sure about the other two..." Bri said, face bent over her phone, trying not to look at Rosalee's scuffle with the shirt.

"You talked to Georgia?" Rosalee asked, breathily. Now she was attempting to stretch out the tight cotton away from her bulging waistline. There had been a time or two when I wondered ... could she be pregnant? In my mind, I'd fantasized about the way she and Asher would break the news to me—a fancy cake with a hidden message inside or a gift that when opened would reveal the grainy ultrasound portrait of my first grandchild...

Rosalee wasn't the daughter-in-law I'd hoped for but having a grandchild on the way ... that would have changed everything. The clock is ticking; I wasn't getting any younger and I hoped to still have some energy for a grand baby someday...

"Yeah. Georgia texted me about an hour ago. She should be here by now," Bri said casually, eyes still glued to her phone.

My eyes wandered over Rosalee's face, the pained expression at the mention of Georgia's name. It made no secret of the fact that I thought it would be Georgia standing here—more toned and better dressed than Rosalee—serving as the bride-to-be for Asher. Asher and Georgia had been thick as thieves since grade school, those two. Georgia's mother and I had been lifelong friends; as children, Asher and Georgia were always running together, keeping themselves entertained with pirate and war games, while Mary and I sipped gin and tonics and gossiped about the men in our lives.

In middle school and high school, Georgia and Asher had developed into miniature adults ... Georgia blossomed and grew prettier, and Asher shot up like a flower, towering over her and all his classmates. He was destined to play sports and, all through school, he made friends wherever he went.

Any girl would have been lucky to have Asher Beake, but he never left Georgia's side. They rode to school together every morning and afternoon. They spent time together on the weekends. For a long time, I just assumed they were dating ... it was only natural ... I didn't even know Rosalee existed back then and I don't think Asher did either...it wasn't until she moved back to town later that I really got to know the girl...

After high school, Asher left for law school and Georgia studied to be a nurse; they drifted apart, and Asher met other women, sometimes bringing them home for breaks or holidays. None of them measured up to Georgia. Not even close.

When Rosalee moved back to town and she and Asher started dating, it became obvious that it was more than a short-lived fling. For some reason that I couldn't quite grasp, my son was enamored by Rosalee. He laughed and smiled every time she was around, and seemed unbothered by her plain, messy appearance.

Finally, I had asked him—what was the deal with Georgia? By then, she was done with nursing school; like Asher, she had come back home to her family and roots. Why were they not pursuing something romantic? Why did he choose the frumpy Rosalee over the girl he'd known all his life, Georgia?

Ah Mom. You know me and Georgia have always just been

friends. *I don't think of her in that way, and she doesn't either,* Asher had said.

But he was wrong—I could see it in Georgia's eyes when he told her the news about Rosalee. Georgia was jealous about his upcoming marriage, she had to be. *I only wish she would try to stop him, stop this whole ridiculous charade before it's too late…*

"There she is! Hello, darling!" I squealed, mustering all the excitement I could. It wasn't hard when it came to Georgia, my greeting totally at odds with how I had greeted Rosalee earlier.

Georgia approached us gracefully, her Coach carry-on in the crook of her arm and an extra-large, matching suitcase rolling beside her. She set her luggage down and opened her arms, embracing me in a too-long hug. She smelled like honeydew and toothpaste; and, as usual, she looked like a girl who, although humbly and smartly dressed, could have been a runway model. Thick blond hair, beachy waves. Long, exotic eyelashes that were clearly extensions, but could probably pass for real ones. When she smiled, she showed all her teeth. And, as I glanced down at her feet, I noted her espadrilles—she had better taste in shoes, that's for sure.

Georgia extracted herself from our embrace and turned to Rosalee. "Hi there! Congratulations! I'm so excited for this trip. Thank you for letting me come, and for asking me to be a bridesmaid." Beaming, Georgia put her arms around Rosalee, who looked startled as she settled into the embrace. That was one thing that Georgia and Rosalee had in common—they were both too nice. *I wish she'd run Rosalee off and stake her claim on my son. Lord knows they look more suited for one another, and they're both enthusiastic about their careers. Unlike Rosalee, with her strange and eerie paintings, the dusty spots of chalk on her clothes and face whenever I stop by for a visit...*

"Aw, it's my pleasure. Thank you for agreeing to be a bridesmaid. You're Asher's best friend, so it only makes sense..." Rosalee said. She closed her mouth then opened it ... then closed it again, as though she had something else to say but couldn't.

As Bri handed over Georgia's shirt—nicer and well-fitted, for certain—I watched Rosalee study my son's best friend. It was no surprise Georgia intimidated her.

Good. She should be intimidated. She should be afraid of us all, I thought, slyly.

Chapter Three

MARA

The best friend

My eyes wandered from one woman to the next as I approached with my shiny black carry-on bag. *I have many flaws, but if there's one thing I'm good at it's reading a room.* Rosalee's awful soon-to-be in-laws, the beak-nosed Mrs. Beake and her thunderous daughter Bri looked downright miserable, waiting in their neatly pressed designer pants, silky button-downs, and over-priced flats. *Did they plan out their outfits together in advance? Ew,* I thought, leerily.

And *Georgia. The* fucking Georgia. Don't get me started on her…

Georgia is the bane of my best friend Rosalee's existence. Rosalee didn't tell me that, but then again, she didn't need to. Best friends know these things.

When your fiancée's "best friend" is a woman who looks like an Instagram model, there's nothing left to do but hate. And, being me, I can't help hating anyone who upsets my closest friend from college.

Call me old-fashioned, but women and men aren't friends. If they are, it's only because one of them wants more and the other doesn't. *Georgia makes no sense to me...*

For the life of me, I couldn't understand it—Rosalee had asked me to be her maid-of-honor (obviously), and I could understand having Tinsley as a bridesmaid too. Tinsley was Rosalee's only cousin and Tinsley's family had taken her in after the tragic loss of her parents. *Me and Tinsley—we make sense—and Tinsley has at least proven herself to be useful, covering most of the party costs on her own. But why did Rosalee have to ask Bri and Georgia to be bridesmaids, too?*

I'd had no choice but to invite the other two bridesmaids to the bachelorette party ... and then Rosalee had also insisted we ask Elizabeth, the matriarch of the Beakes, with her poufy white hair and long nose, perfect to look down on you with...

Frankly, my best friend was being way too nice. The party was supposed to be about her, *for her* ... not a way to kiss up to her future in-laws and her husband's female "bestie". If I'd have had it my way, we would have invited our closest acquaintances from our college days and had a wild shindig, stress-free.

But Rosalee wanted this, and as the party thrower, it was my job to meet her demands.

I was determined to make this bachelorette party not only a weekend to remember, but the best fucking weekend of Rosalee's life.

My best friend is getting married, and she deserves this. She deserves to feel celebrated. I just wish she would have chosen some kinder participants...

Rosalee looked so awkward and unsure of herself standing in that group of women; I just wanted to squeeze her up and dropkick those bitches around her. Especially Georgia.

"Ladies!" I launched my bag toward their inner circle and slid my owlish sunglasses down my nose. "Who's ready for the best fucking weekend of their life?"

Elizabeth's mouth fell open and Bri narrowed her eyes at me. And I didn't even bother looking at Georgia. Lord knows I'd studied her enough on the Gram already.

"Elizabeth and Bri! So lovely to finally meet Asher's family in person!" I squealed with mock delight.

Elizabeth offered me a matronly hand; her wedding ring sparkled like a firecracker, gaudy yet wonderful. I hated her for it. Ignoring the hand, I reached for my best friend's future mother-in-law, and squeezed her perfectly narrowed waistline so hard she let out a small "umph". As much as it killed me to admit it, Elizabeth Beake was hot for an old lady. She dressed to impress in sharp clothes and expensive jewels, putting off old money vibes without even trying to.

Bri, the sister, was big and brutish, too hard to get my arms around. But she was well-dressed and expensively dressed like her mother. I gave her a light hug with a hard slap on the back. Despite the plastered smile, her face was disdainful. These Beake women were exuding *hate vibes* … I could see why they intimidated Rosalee.

Lucky for me, I don't get shaken so easily.

Next, I turned to Georgia. "Ummm … I'm so sorry. It's early and I haven't had my coffee. Joanna, right?"

"Georgia," Elizabeth snapped before Georgia could even answer.

"Georgia, Georgia…!" I belted out the words to that timeless Ray Charles song, startling a few huffy travelers passing by. "I bet you hear that all the time, right?" I teased.

When Georgia smiled, it was like her whole face smiled with her. Her eyes were pale green, her face dewy and smooth as a skincare commercial, her lips soft and small like a perfect rosebud. Even though I hated to admit it, this one exuded *sweetness*.

"Oh, you wouldn't believe how often people start singing my name! When I was younger, I found it annoying, but now it's kind of endearing. It is a good song, after all. They could always sing something worse, I guess..." Georgia said.

"Right. Like, 'Jolene, Jolene, Jolene...'" I belted, clapping out the beat on my thigh with one hand.

If Georgia caught my drift, she didn't show it. Instead, she said, "Well, it's awfully nice to meet Rosalee's best friend. Finally! Asher's told me so much about you."

Asher, huh?

"Hopefully only the good things," I said, turning toward my best friend. *Why is Georgia talking to Asher about me? Sure, I've spent some time with Rosalee's fiancé, but it's not like he knows me all that well either...*

"Come here, you." I took my best friend in my arms, squeezing and tugging until I'd lifted her off her feet. "Wait. What the hell is this? Did they order a kid's size by accident?" I let her go and tugged on that disastrous bridal party shirt. Bri had insisted on being in charge of the shirts. But I knew this would happen. Luckily, I'd come prepared.

"Oh, it's not so bad. It's cute, just a little tight..." Rosalee tugged at the waist, trying to stretch the material out around her stomach.

"Oh, now you're just being nice! It's definitely too

small and looks cheaply made, too. I guess it could be worse. At least they didn't accidentally pick up a maternity size!" I let out a loud, raucous chuckle, then turned to lock eyes with Elizabeth. *Yes, of course my best friend told me about the maternity debacle at Christmas. And yes, I predicted that you and your daughter wouldn't do a respectable job with the shirts today, either...*

"Don't worry, sweetie, I picked up some gorgeous black and purple pre-made shirts at Barney's last weekend. I have one for you right here in my bag. Let's go to the bathroom and take that one off..."

Rosalee's cheeks turned apple-red.

"Come on," I insisted. Locking arms, I steered her in the direction of the airport bathrooms.

Over my shoulder, I flipped a look at Bri, beaming her with my best "fuck you, bitch" smile.

They can try all they want to ruin my best friend's party and her impending marriage, but I won't let them. Nobody is hurting Rosalee this weekend, unless it's over my dead body...

"Thank you," Rosalee muttered, once we were safely tucked in the stall. She lifted the too-tight shirt over her head as I unfolded the new one and handed it to her. She seemed tense and distracted, her shoulders and jaw tight. Her eyes far away and sleepy. *Was it just the drama and anxiety of dealing with her in-laws or was it something more?* There was a stiffness to her that I hadn't seen in a long time, like she was going through the motions but not really present...

"Are you okay? I'm sorry about the shirt. I should have insisted on doing that myself too..."

"I'm fine." Rosalee slid the new purple shirt over her head and adjusted her stubby black ponytail.

I shoved the other shirt in the tampon can, watching my best friend's reflection in the bathroom mirror. She lifted her lips, trying to force a smile. Watching her made me feel a sudden rush of sadness.

"Lucky in love", the shirt read, the 'o' fashioned into a glittery engagement ring. *But was she truly lucky?* I couldn't help wondering. *Yes, she's marrying the guy she's coveted since grade school, but is it worth it if she has to deal with those terrible in-laws?*

"You sure you're okay? Was everything fine with Asher when you left?" I reached up and adjusted her ponytail for her in the mirror. One thing I loved about Rosalee—she was never fake, and she liked to dress for comfort. *Sure, she could dress up more from time to time and she's put on a few extra pounds since getting engaged, but she will always be a hottie in my book. Screw those mean bitches for trying to ruin her day from the get-go!*

"Yeah. Everything's fine. But where is Tinsley? I figured y'all would show up together since you planned the party together..." Rosalee said, shifting out of my grasp.

I took a deep breath through my mouth and blew it out like a bull through my nose. I'd been dreading this moment. "Yeah, about that ... Tinsley isn't coming. I'm sorry."

Chapter Four

TINSLEY

The cousin

It's not that I'm afraid of flying. I just don't like the crowds or the claustrophobia, stuck with all those tightly compacted bodies 40,000 feet in the air.

If anyone could understand my fears, it was my cousin Rosalee. We had practically grown up together as sisters, her coming to live with me and my mother at the age of fourteen after her parents died.

The drive to New Orleans was grueling, but I'd relished the time alone in my Prius, listening to audiobooks and blasting my favorite old songs from the nineties. Not only did I make it on time, but by the time I backed into my long-term parking slot, I was hours early.

A shiny black Uber was there waiting to pick me up.

"What's going on? You must be Tinsley," the driver said with a big flashy smile, rolling his window all the way down. It wasn't my first time visiting The Big Easy, but I'd forgotten the beauty of its accents—this man's vowels round and smooth like cobbles in a stream.

"That's me. Let me grab my bag." I double and triple checked my door locks, then switched my luggage over to his car.

"Let me get that for you. On in." He opened the back door for me, and I slid in, grateful for the air conditioning and the soft, cool seats. *It might have taken me half a night and day's drive to get here, but at least I avoided the plane and all those people. I just hope Rosalee wasn't too disappointed.*

The drive had been strange, chilly temperatures fading away when I reached Birmingham, and the moisture thickening as I drew further south. The air in New Orleans felt sticky and airless, settling over my skin like a layer of soup.

"What brings you to New Orleans?" he asked, although when he said it, it sounded like "Nyoo Ahhlyins". I smiled politely at his bright white teeth in the rearview.

"Bachelorette party for my cousin. Though she's more like a sister really…"

"Ah! You missed Mardi Gras. Too bad," he said, pulling away from my Prius. As he swooped into traffic onto a busy, colorful street, I watched my car disappear through the rearview mirror.

"Yeah, too bad. My cousin, Rosalee … she wanted to avoid the carnival crowds," I said. Mardi Gras was over, but you couldn't tell it—beads still clung to porch rails and remnants of bright awnings, balloons, and streamers were displayed on the houses and shops. The sidewalks were busy with people, some dressed as brightly as the colorful buildings beside them.

Awestruck, I watched the multi-colored buildings swish by—there was no separation between them, as though the entire city were connected, one long heaping heart, each artery pumping blood to the next chamber.

Perhaps it was age that helped me see it clearer now; I was barely twenty-one when I came here last, and the whole place looked different now. The Gothic-inspired moldings and lacy wrought iron; the shotguns next to the Creole cottages … this amazing patchwork of French, Spanish, and Caribbean influences meshed into this unbelievable tapestry. *There's no other place quite like it, that's for sure.*

"Leblanc and Landry, right?" the driver asked, breaking the spell that had overcome me.

"That's the one." The Leblanc-Landry Mansion was in the Garden district, close enough to Bourbon Street and the festivities of downtown, but also with an air of seclusion on its acre of land, surrounded by tremendous old oak trees.

Mara and I had pored over the pictures dozens of times, planning and planning. Well, it was mostly her—I just nodded and went along with whatever she said. I'd quickly learned that there was no "team" in teamwork with Rosalee's best friend Mara; she ran the show and you either assisted or got the hell out of her way.

Leblanc-Landry was secluded and romantic, with its hidden courtyard, freakish old trees, and cotton candy architecture—it was perfect, all but the price. When I'd agreed to help plan Rosalee's bachelorette party, I hadn't agreed to foot the bill.

Mara had promised to pay me back before the trip— I'd put most of it on my credit card. But here I was, in New Orleans ... and she still hadn't paid me. Mara, with all her trendy clothes and accessories ... the pricey make-up and designer haircut ... without a dollar to her name, apparently. There were so many excuses—she needed to "move some money around first"; she was waiting for an owed payment from her employer; she lent too much to her sick relatives...

I'd heard it all from Mara over the last few months. At first, I'd been inclined to believe her. But then she never paid me back. And despite running up the bill in my name, she spared no expense for the party, either.

Let's face it. I'll probably be stuck with my three nearly maxed out credit cards while Mara gets all the credit for the party from Rosalee and the other attendees...

Unlike Mara, I wasn't a college kid with a trust fund or a degree to fall back on. I had to work for every penny I earned at my job, and her thoughtlessness when it came to paying me back was enough to make me clench my teeth every time I conjured up her face or name...

I took a deep breath, counting backwards ... forcing myself to push aside the thought of money for this one weekend, to focus on my dear cousin Rosalee. We had practically grown up together, sharing so many moments and memories ... and it was hard to believe she was getting married.

Closing my eyes, I could see us there, fourteen and fabulous, wrapping our bodies in sheets and fashioning tiaras out of weeds from my mother's garden. We held fake wedding ceremonies and chanted whimsical vows, playacting adulthood.

Oh, if only adulthood were as fun and easy and magical as we made it seem back then...

The hodgepodge heartbeat of the city grew softer as the buildings and townhouses faded away. Around a sharp bend and over a small hill, I saw the mansion. It was set back from the road, a massive bleeding heart at the end of a crooked lane. Even from here, I could see the statues and decorations we had ordered for the party on display in the carriageway. Excuse me—the décor that *I* paid for, not Mara.

The driver flipped his signal and turned down the long driveway.

"So, what are your all's plans for the weekend? Going to get wild?" the driver asked, his eyes watchful and animalistic in the rearview mirror.

"No ... I don't know. I'm sure we'll visit some local nightspots and get a feel of the city," I said, tearing my eyes away from his and looking eagerly toward the mansion approaching.

"Well, why don't you and your friends call my number if you need a ride? Or if you're looking to party, me and some of my boys can come by. A big mansion like that, you got plenty of room for a big party," the driver said.

"If you don't mind," I said, placing my hand on the handle, "I think I'll get out and walk from here. If it's okay with you..."

"You sure? I don't mind carrying your bag inside ... especially considering the generous tip..."

"No, that won't be necessary. I'd like to take the walk and carry my own bags," I insisted, eager to escape from him. "Thank you so much for bringing me though." I'd left a tip for him on the Uber app, but I handed him an extra twenty and forced a smile.

"Don't forget what I said. I can show you ladies a good time," he said, glancing at the mansion as though he might try to come inside right now.

"Okay. Sure." I took the business card he was offering and hopped out.

"Thanks again ... Henry," I said, glancing at the card, then slammed my door shut with a thud.

After collecting my bag, I watched Henry pull away. *I definitely won't be calling him for a ride again*, I thought, with a small shudder.

I turned to look at the mansion, relieved that I was all alone again. It was a beautiful place, in an eclectic, other-worldly way, although I would have gone without the cheesy decorations strewn out front if it were up to me instead of domineering Mara.

I approached slowly, bag swinging beside me, taking in the massive trees, most of which were between 600 and 900 years old. I'd done my research on this place online. While Mara was busy worrying about the linens, culinary delicacies, and amenities, I was reading everything I could on the Leblanc-Landry estate.

There were stories and rumors about this place ... voodoo and murder. But there were many places like that in New Orleans. The difference with this one was that it was supposedly haunted. A couple of amateur ghost-hunting crews from YouTube had turned out years ago, catching some interesting footage for their channel.

Most normal people would shy away from this place ... I know Mara certainly would if she knew. *But I'm not normal. I'm not most people. The dark and macabre attract me ... and this place has been speaking to me ever since I first laid eyes on the grainy photos online.*

Some of the ghost hunters called this place "evil". But when you grow up in the buckle of the Bible Belt, you're taught to fear fire and brimstone before you're even out of diapers, nothing scares you anymore.

This house ... it feels like the perfect place to reconnect with Rosalee and make sure she wants to marry this man. And while I'm here, why not enjoy the creepy location, too? Perhaps I could catch a ghost sighting or two of my own and submit it to my favorite YouTubers...

The pearls and beads strewn over the awning were pretty and tasteful, but I scowled at the overgrown bride and groom. Facing each other on either side of the entranceway steps, their faces were puckered ... not as though they were preparing to kiss, but rather holding their breath, as though caught in the middle of a tense argument...

I knocked on the heavy French doors, wondering if I was too early. The caterers and support staff were scheduled to arrive before the bride-to-be and her group, but they probably hadn't expected me to turn up three hours early.

I knocked again, then placed my hand on the brass doorknob. The door creaked open, startling me.

"Hello?" I popped my head around the door but saw no one on the other side of it. Stepping inside, I closed the door behind me and set my suitcase on the floor against the foyer wall.

The foyer was dark. No natural light seeping in, the windows high and foggy, despite the late afternoon hour. Candles burned on either side of the entry, casting wavy glows from their sconces, making the eccentric oil paintings and designs on the aging wallpaper look strange and menacing.

"Hello?" I called out again, my voice ricocheting through a long dark hallway. I followed the candlelight, gasping as I entered a grand ballroom—no, not a ballroom, a dining room. The long-slabbed table and high-backed chairs reminded me of something medieval; a table fit for a king and his retinue.

Finally, I heard noises—the clank of metal on glass, the sizzle of someone cooking. I followed the symphony of sounds, finding my way through two metal swinging doors that led to an industrial-sized kitchen. Half a dozen chefs were hard at work, rolling dough for desserts, bowling crab legs, slicing vegetables and cheese for salads.

"Hello! You must be Mara!"

I jumped at the sound of a voice beside me, turning quickly to an elderly, stout woman dressed all in black. She was wearing a shiny gold nametag. *Delfina.*

"No, I'm Tinsley. Mara is the other friend planning the party." I stuck out my hand and she took it.

"Tinsley … I don't think we've spoken. It's mostly been Mara, going back and forth in our email exchanges…"

I frowned. "Yes, that's right. Of the two of us, she's definitely the one in charge of handling communication. But I'm the one footing the bill." I couldn't resist letting her know.

"Oh." Delfina shifted her matronly hips and gave me an uncomfortable smile. She looked like Betty Crocker, with her old-fashioned apron and starch-white uniform. She had to be nearly seventy or eighty years old…

"The others flew, but I drove. I'm sorry if I arrived too early. I just couldn't help myself … this place is simply marvelous," I breathed, watching the workers float effortlessly around the kitchen as though they were following a carefully choreographed dance.

"Oh, no problem at all!" Delfina grinned. "We are so grateful to have you. We get so many revelers and tourists during Mardi Gras. It's nice to have a proper party to tend to. I'm pleased to have you," she said curtly, with a practiced smile. She seemed friendly but proper, and I could tell that she was the one in charge by the way she watched the others moving through the kitchen with a hawklike stance.

"Well, thank you for letting us do it here and agreeing to host the dinner. How can I help?"

Delfina waved me off. "No need for anything. I have it all taken care of. The bedrooms are on the second floor. Each room has been pre-selected, and you should easily find yours. Dinner will be served at seven, not a moment sooner…"

"Thanks again, Delfina."

Once outside the kitchen, I went back and retrieved my suitcase. But instead of going up to the bedrooms, I wandered around the first-floor rooms. The dining and sitting rooms were better lit than the entrance, vintage chandeliers glittering like diamonds in every room I passed. Everything looked clean, but vintage—the heavy cream curtains, the weird portraits, odd ceramic sculptures, and knickknacks spread in every open crevice and corner.

Through the back window, I could see the pavilion—a cobbled courtyard filled with wrought iron café tables, bright yellow string lights strewn through the trees and along the brick archways … like its own little slice of Paris. It was still daylight, yet the lights were on, the secluded brick barriers giving it a dark, intimate feel.

Through an archway, I could see the part of the estate

that had Mara's name written all over it. An inground pool surrounded by modern loungers, and a steamy hot tub under a palm tree and surrounded by thick, private shrubs. *I didn't even realize there were palm trees in New Orleans,* I thought, dreamily.

This place truly was an odd mixture of old and new, strange and familiar ... sort of like the exterior designs of the house and surrounding city. A city where you go to feel connected, found. But at the same time, it seemed like the sort of place where you could blend in and, eventually, disappear if you wanted to. Outside Mardi Gras, there was no separation between tourists and locals —just a blending of peoples.

I shook away my thoughts, feeling strangely sleepy. *Perhaps I'll lie down and rest a bit before the others arrive...*

But on the way to the grand second-floor staircase, I ran into more distractions.

Jaw-dropping chandeliers and a fancy bathroom bigger than my bedroom back home, fitted with pedestal sinks and more chandeliers inside it.

A lavish sunroom filled with Turkish rugs and well-worn but well-loved sofas and loveseats.

I stopped and took a short breath when I found the library.

"Jesus Christ." The walls were lined floor to ceiling with heavy books. In the center of the room were several leather reading chairs and tiny tables that offered old-fashioned glass ashtrays. *If this were my library, I'd kill someone for smoking in it,* I thought, peevishly.

The books were also vintage—Dickens and Twain. Shakespeare and Faulkner. As much as I loved the old-worldly feel of this place, I felt like the books were trying too hard. *There's nothing wrong with classics, but if this were my library, I'd fill it with new, modern titles. Feminist and edgy ... I'd put every banned book I could find on the lowest and easiest to reach shelves...*

I was tempted to borrow a book or two, but they were so perfectly arranged, it would certainly be noticeable if I did so. *I'll ask Delfina later. Maybe the books can be checked out somehow, or at the very least I could park myself right here in this room when I need a break from the others and could do some reading in one of those luxurious chairs...*

My eyes grew heavier just thinking about it, the exhaustion from the long drive and the overly pushy driver bearing down on my shoulders and chest. My eyelids felt weighty as I made my way back out through the long dark hallway and up the double-sided staircase that led to the second-floor bedrooms.

The second floor was less grand than the first, but I preferred it—the walls painted a soft, eggshell blue at the bottom, curly bits of flower and ivy wallpaper stretching to meet the ceiling above. Precisely six bedrooms—it couldn't be a more perfect set-up for Rosalee's bachelorette party. Almost as though we were destined to come here...

Through the long, airy hallway, I peeked in, room by room, looking for mine. As planned, each private room came equipped with its own lush bathrobe on the bed, each guest's name stitched in gold lettering on the right breast. *I wonder how much each of these cost me*, I thought, bitterly, rolling my eyes when I saw the one with Mara's name etched in gold. *I don't understand what Rosalee sees in Mara, I truly don't. She's self-centered and annoying.* But that wasn't true—unlike me, with my hermit-like tendencies and withdrawn personality, Rosalee could shine in a crowd. She knew how to fake it; in fact, I'd watched her do it for years after her parents died. *And an outgoing person like Mara was exactly the type of friend Rosalee had always been drawn to...*

Rosalee was fourteen when she came to live with me and my mother. To say I wanted her there would be an epic lie. I didn't want her to come at all.

Rosalee's father was my mother's brother, but I'd only met them once previously, before that fateful day when Rosalee lost both mother and father in the span of a few short hours.

Mom didn't ask me if it was okay; rather, she told me that Rosalee was coming. Not to stay for a while, but to live permanently. And she expected me to treat her with care. *I want you to do better than kindness, Tinsley. I want you to shower her with love. Make her feel at home. Just think of her as the sister you always wanted but never had*, my mother insisted.

But that's just it—I'd never wanted a sister either.

Dad died of a stroke when I was six; my memories of him were mostly non-existent. A stick-figure man whom I filled in myself, each time making him fuller and more colorful, and over time, my imagination altered the course of my memories forever.

When you lose someone at that age, your memory of them—your idea of them, really—is just a hodgepodge of other people's stories. His old bomber jackets in the coat closet; the smell of tobacco and Old Spice embedded in the fabrics tucked in the dark corner boxes in the basement. Pictures … so many of them. Just a face and a body; no one I knew, not really.

For as far back as I could remember, it was just my mom and me. We lived alone in our three-bedroom townhouse; we ate easy meals together, like grilled cheese and tomato soup, or pink salmon from a can.

I enjoyed our dinners. Tucked away at our two-seater table or curled up thigh to thigh on the loveseat watching old episodes of *Cheers* or *The Brady Bunch*.

Occasionally, I complained of boredom. I made few friends and Mom made even fewer in her grown-up world, working at the local mortuary. *My co-workers are a bunch of stiffs*, she would say at school functions, a recycled joke for the other parents—a punchline no one seemed to understand or appreciate. But I did.

Honestly, I wasn't all that bored. I enjoyed her company at that age more than I cared to admit. Mostly, I enjoyed the company of my books, tucked away in my room. My idea of an epic weekend was reading mom's old Harlequin romance novels or classic mysteries.

So, when Rosalee Mumford moved into our house, blood or not, I was annoyed by her presence. She was like Stella Starr from *Space Invaders*, this sexy marauder with her full breasts to my flat chest, her wild drawings and painting habits ... her abhorrence for reading.

I hated her those first few days. We had a spare room she could have used, but Mom insisted on keeping that space to herself for sewing and praying ... so after a lifetime of living as an only child with my own space, my room was suddenly rearranged. Bunk beds and an extra dresser. Half the normal space for my clothes and, most importantly, my precious books.

But something happened that first summer with Rosalee... We might have been different, our personalities ... but we connected in a way I'd never anticipated.

She had dreams ... nightmares really. And after a few nights of tossing and turning, screams and shouts ... she asked if she could get in bed with me. I guess most people would have thought it was strange—two fourteen-year-old girls crowded together on a twin-sized mattress. I certainly thought it was strange at first.

But for the first time since her arrival, Rosalee had slept. She curled her calves around mine, like interlocking pieces, and I watched her breathing, short puffy breaths that made her curlicue bangs float out when she exhaled.

My cousin was beautiful. And damaged. I couldn't imagine losing my mother. Sure, I'd lost Dad, but I'd been too young to feel it. To understand it fully at the time.

Late night sleeping sessions became late night confessions. Rosalee told me her secrets and I told her mine. I read her pages from my stories, and she painted a picture of me, making me look beautiful in a way I'd never seen or felt before.

We spent the daytime hours outdoors, walking to the public pool or park. Riding bikes. I'd never really had a friend before. But more than that—she felt like a sister, just like Mom had said.

I expected it all to change when school started. And in a way, things did evolve.

Rosalee wasn't considered the prettiest girl, but she was new and had lost something, and that intrigued people. Plus, Rosalee was always nice. She fitted in with both boys and girls alike.

Despite all that, she never left my side. She never

made me feel like a leper. The kids at school, in turn, were kinder, including me along with Rosalee.

Middle school advanced to high school. Rosalee joined drama and I joined nothing, spending my free time reading and writing. Mom pushed me to join more things like Rosalee, but Rosalee defended me. *I wish I were smart and had the patience for reading like Tinsley. If I did, I wouldn't be running around trying to find extra things to keep me busy,* she told her.

The closer I got to Rosalee and my school friends, the farther I got from Mom. I guess that's what happens when you become a teenager. Things change, and maybe they're supposed to.

I didn't know Mom had cancer; she knew but never told us, and to this day, I feel angry at her for not giving me a chance to deal with it, to say some sort of formal goodbye…

Rosalee and I were both nearly eighteen by then; a distant uncle we barely knew on my father's side came to stay with us for a brief time. Rosalee left for college, and I spent my days missing my mother. And I missed Rosalee, too.

I thought it would be me … going off to study, to write books or get a degree in library science. But it was Rosalee who left town, and I was the one who stayed. Left behind with Uncle Noah. I got a job at the local bookstore and tried my best to cope with depression and grief. I missed Mom so terribly, and although I'd never admit it to anyone, I missed Rosalee even more.

We stayed in contact—phone calls and texts. A few letters. But it wasn't the same.

I became a full-fledged adult and Uncle Noah moved out. All that was left was me and all those empty rooms, the ghosts of my mother and pseudo-sister to keep me company.

When Rosalee finally finished college and moved back to Moon County, she didn't come home to me. She got her own apartment. Things just weren't the same between us. She had brand new friends, like Mara.

Perhaps part of me resented her for that—for pulling me away from my mom, holding me in her orbit for so long, and then flinging me out into space all by myself when she was done with me.

I never did go to college. For one, I couldn't afford it. Rosalee had a small inheritance from her parents' death and took out some hardship loans that I never even considered applying for myself.

I just kept working and living, going through the motions of life. Wishing I could turn the tables, turn back the clock for a little while…

Now, this weekend was an opportunity for me to reconnect with my beloved cousin. *Mara might be her best friend, but she doesn't know Rosalee like I do. She doesn't know her secrets. And she doesn't know that this whole thing is a charade … Rosalee will never be happy with Asher. There are too many things she keeps hidden from him and no successful marriage starts out on a mountain of lies…*

The Bachelorette Party is available in ebook and paperback now

YOUR NUMBER ONE STOP

ONE MORE CHAPTER

FOR PAGETURNING BOOKS

One More Chapter is an
award-winning global
division of HarperCollins.

Sign up to our newsletter to get our
latest eBook deals and stay up to date
with our weekly Book Club!
<u>Subscribe here.</u>

Meet the team at
<u>www.onemorechapter.com</u>

Follow us!
🐦 <u>@OneMoreChapter_</u>
f <u>@OneMoreChapter</u>
📷 <u>@onemorechapterhc</u>

Do you write unputdownable fiction?
We love to hear from new voices.
Find out how to submit your novel at
<u>www.onemorechapter.com/submissions</u>